A WHISPER IN THE WIND

JEK

B. J. HOFF

LIFEJOURNEY
BOOKS

LifeJourney Books™ is an imprint of Chariot Family Publishing,
a div. of David C. Cook Publishing Co.
David C. Cook Publishing Co., Elgin, Illinois 60120
David C. Cook Publishing Co., Weston, Ontario
Nova Distribution Ltd., Newton Abbot, England

A WHISPER IN THE WIND
© 1987, 1993 by B. J. Hoff

Cover design by Turnbaugh & Associates
Interior design by Glass House Graphics
Editing by Penelope Stokes

First Revised Printing, 1993
Printed in the United States of America
96 95 94 93 5 4 3 2 1

Library of Congress Catalog Card Number 87-70529
ISBN 0-78140-407-X

For Jim,
For Mother,
For Dana and Jessie. . .
Bail ó Dhia ort

PROLOGUE

Washington, D.C., 1845

I t's absolutely imperative that Dalton never know of your association with us." The cold, thin voice belonged to a man of great influence and small conscience—a man with the power to make presidents, wreck careers, create laws, and destroy lives.

"I understand, sir." The reply came from a dark-haired young man with a dream, an ambition, and a secret.

"You know what's expected of you?"

"Yes, sir, I do. I'm to advise you of his movements and how our strategies appear to be affecting him. Should he vary his routine significantly or react in a way we haven't anticipated, I will inform you at once." He blinked his dark eyes rapidly as he recited the words by rote.

The older man nodded and lightly drummed his well-manicured fingertips on the surface of his desk. "Very well. Your research would seem to be thorough. It's perfectly obvious the only weapon we have is his wife. Threatening Dalton himself would be futile, a total waste of time."

5

"Yes, sir. He seems to be entirely without fear for himself. But he's absolutely besotted with the woman."

"A common enough affliction—and a definite weakness. All right; we'll begin immediately. His wife arrives tomorrow?"

"Yes. Midafternoon."

The man behind the enormous desk brushed at the lapel of his exquisitely tailored suit and rose from his chair, a signal that he was about to dismiss his informant. "Dalton will be gone when she arrives?"

The younger man quickly stood. "That's all been taken care of, sir. He'll be in Baltimore. He's asked the church caretaker to meet his wife at the train station and drive her to the parsonage. She'll be alone in the house at least until evening."

"Excellent." He studied the narrow, swarthy face opposite him for a moment, his eyes frigid and unreadable. "Before you go, I want to be sure you're perfectly clear as to the importance of this . . . effort . . . to my people—and to your future."

The slender youth moistened his lips and swallowed hard. "Yes, sir."

The impeccably groomed middle-aged man walked around his desk. "Of course you are. Do your job well, and your . . . problem . . . will cease to exist. In addition, you will assure your success in the political arena. Fail—" He paused meaningfully. "And you'll spend the rest of your life as a lackey—a disgraced lackey." He smiled, a brief, chilling slash. "I want you to know that I have the fullest confidence in you."

"Yes, sir. Thank you, sir." Certain he was dismissed, he hurried from the office.

The man walked with easy grace to his office window and turned his aristocratic features out on the city. *My city*, he thought, lifting his chin arrogantly. *Washington. The very word is synonymous with power.* His eyes shone with a glint approximating lust. *This is where our manifest destiny is actually born—where it's designed and planned and charted. He tightened his jaw. And no abolitionist pulpit pounder is going to come in and start tearing down what I've worked for years to build!*

CHAPTER ONE

A barrel-chested carriage driver with a thick walrus mustache lumbered down from his seat and helped his passenger out of the carriage.

"Here we are then, missus," he announced soberly, lifting her small valise from the back of the carriage. "Safe and sound at the parsonage, just as the pastor instructed." He tucked the valise under his arm and started briskly up the walk, stopping just long enough to open the iron gate for Kerry, who could barely keep up with his long-legged stride.

As she scurried along behind him, Kerry stared at his broad, perspiration-stained back with a prickle of irritation. She would have preferred a leisurely first look at her new home. Instead, she was forced to take in as much detail as possible while they hurried along.

Her peevish mood wasn't the fault of the taciturn driver. Perhaps it was the result of the oppressive August heat. Jess had been right; he'd warned her that Washington's muggy summer temperatures were drastically different from the brisk fresh air of West Point. In addition, the rough carriage ride from the railway station had taken its toll; Kerry was feeling definitely squeamish.

But then, her stomach had been somewhat undependable for several months now. Making an effort to smooth her rumpled skirt, she discreetly touched her rounded abdomen.

"Ah, my little love, just you be patient a bit longer now," she murmured. "We'll soon be having us a proper rest. And best of all, your da will be joining us before the night ends."

Unable to keep up with the driver any longer, Kerry deliberately stopped to catch her breath a few feet from the porch. She tilted her head back and gazed up at the giant oaks that stood like matched sentries guarding the house. The highest branches from one tree searched out branches from the other. Where they met, they entwined like giant tentacles and formed a massive arch that framed the house.

Kerry remembered the description they'd received a few weeks ago from one of the deacons. It made the parsonage sound impressively attractive. She supposed it was a grand enough dwelling, looking at it from the outside. It was far more elegant than the average parsonage, Jess had written in one of his first letters to her. There was even a brick carriage house off to the side. And hadn't Jess mentioned a pond and a caretaker's cottage in back? Why then did she find its stately appearance oddly intimidating, even sinister?

Startled by her own thoughts, she felt an icy rivulet of fear creep down her spine. *Sure, and the heat is working on my brain,* she thought, glancing at the overcast sky. The driver had mentioned an approaching summer storm; now she could feel the stifling closeness in the air as the sky grew dark with low, threatening clouds.

Returning to her study of the parsonage, Kerry noticed that the old red bricks were in good condition, as were the black shutters framing the long, narrow windows. Perhaps it was only the untended shrubbery and randomly scattered enormous old trees that made the property appear neglected; for, in truth, the house itself seemed to have had good care.

She gave her flower-trimmed bonnet a gentle tug, allowing it to fall and hang idly about her neck by its ribbons while she removed her white silk gloves. A slight breeze stirred; she sighed with relief.

"I'll just unlock the house for you, missus, and then bring in the rest of your luggage," the man said, not meeting her gaze.

Murtagh Mackenzie was his name, he'd told her at the railway station, introducing himself as caretaker of both the church and the parsonage. That had been his only attempt at conversation, and even it was made with seeming reluctance.

Kerry offered him a weak smile, puffed her way up the steps to the white-pillared porch, and followed him through the door. He set her valise in a corner of the large, paneled reception hall and shambled back outside to get the rest of her things from the carriage. While she waited for him to return, Kerry appraised the dark, formal hall.

Its parquet floor was clean and unmarred, and the rich walnut paneling had been rubbed to a satin sheen. For some reason, though, she found the room funereal.

A finely carved staircase flanked the reception area. She studied it with awed appreciation while Mackenzie brought in her luggage and carried it upstairs.

"Why, this place is a veritable mansion, it is!" she said aloud as her gaze followed the line of the intricately scrolled balusters upward. "Wait until Molly sees that stairway—and all this lovely wood!" For a moment she forgot her initial feelings of disenchantment, thinking instead of the way her housekeeper's eyes would bug when she walked into the reception hall.

When Mackenzie returned, he handed her a large ring of keys. "Will you be needing anything else for now, missus?"

"No, thank you, Mr. Mackenzie. Oh, but I must pay you, of course."

He shook his head vigorously. "No need for that, missus. The pastor has hired me for part-time work." He started out the door, pushed his cap onto his head, then turned. "Most folks just call me Mack or Mackenzie."

The large man nearly filled the doorway, and his stern face refused to soften even a trace. Still, Kerry believed she saw a glimpse of kindness in his dark gray eyes. She smiled warmly at him. "Then I shall be seeing you often—Mackenzie—if you're going to be working for us. I'm certainly obliged to you for meeting me in Jess's—the pastor's absence."

9

"Good day for now, missus. And welcome to Washington, I'm sure." He lifted his cap and immediately set it back onto his balding head.

"Ah . . . Mackenzie?"

He half turned from outside the door. His spectacles slipped downward a notch over the wide bridge of his nose, and he pushed them up into place with his index finger.

"I'm Irish, too, you know."

"Yes, missus," he replied gravely.

Kerry decided she would make him smile before he left the house. "And our housekeeper, Molly Larkin—she'll be arriving in just a few days—she's from Ireland also. She appears to be quite fierce, but she's not at all. I'm sure the two of you will get along very well indeed."

He nodded, his expression never changing.

"Well," Kerry said uncertainly, "I suppose you need to be going then?"

"Aye, that I do. If you'd be needing any help before the pastor arrives this evening, my house is out back. I'll be working over at the church for a bit, but no more than an hour or two."

Pleased, for this was his lengthiest conversation since they'd met, Kerry smiled at him again. "Thank you, Mackenzie. It's a relief to know I can call on you."

Once more he lifted his cap and turned to go.

Finally alone, Kerry stood unmoving in the reception hall for a moment. Then she began to walk slowly toward the parlor, her short, hesitant footsteps echoing about her.

Just inside the doorway she stopped, studying with some misgiving the darkly shadowed room. The parlor was austere to the point of being bleak.

She suddenly wished that Jess had chosen to stay here at the parsonage during the three weeks they'd been apart rather than at a hotel. *I'd not be having these creepy feelings,* she thought, *if the place had been more recently lived in—especially by my Jess.*

Kerry also wished, even more fervently, that he was here with her this very moment so she could lean into his tall, unflinching strength, instead of standing here uneasy and uncertain.

It had been a terrible disappointment, being met at the railway station by Mackenzie instead of by Jess. The burly Irishman had informed her, in as few words as possible, that Jess had been prevailed upon by the family of one of his parishioners to accompany them to a burial service in Baltimore.

Kerry had come close to tears but brightened quickly when she learned that Jess would be returning to Washington that evening. Mackenzie had given her a note from Jess, filled with his regrets and assurances that he'd meet her at the parsonage that evening with "far more eagerness than decency allows me to admit . . ." How she longed for him to come sweeping through that massive front door and gather her into his strong, protective arms. He would dip his head down and whisper a soft, intimate greeting of love, just as he had each evening at their house at West Point.

With a firm shake of her head, Kerry dismissed her reverie and turned her attention to the parlor. Its paneled walls were a dark gray, well kept but depressing. Its widely planked floor was highly polished and protected only by a worn but still serviceable Aubusson. Each correctly placed piece of furniture looked stiff and uncomfortable and only intensified Kerry's initial impression of grim formality. With great resolve, she walked briskly across the room to open the dark velvet drapes, allowing the dim outside light to filter through the room.

A sudden, cold touch of warning caused her to whirl around from the window. "Jess?" She waited, listening, half-expecting to see someone else in the room. She knew she was being foolish, yet she felt gripped by dread. "Is someone here?"

Her voice sounded ridiculously childlike, she thought. *And why not?* she scolded herself angrily. *I'm behaving like a wee wane!*

Swallowing with difficulty, Kerry made a brave attempt to submerge the fear battering at her stomach. She wondered anxiously if the babe she was carrying could sense her terror. For that very reason, she must get herself under control. She must not endanger the child, especially with superstitious nonsense.

She was uncomfortably reminded of Dr. Green's words when he'd put her to bed this last time, no more than a week before Jess had left for Washington to assume his pastorate: "I'm not trying to frighten you, Mrs. Dalton, and I'm certain there's no need

11

to be overly concerned so long as you take care. However, this is the third time you've experienced these pains. I believe we must consider them to be warnings. From now on, you simply must refrain from even the slightest form of exertion. You'll have to spend most of your remaining four months in bed, I'm afraid. There's simply no help to be had for it."

The doctor had given Kerry his permission to travel to Washington only after realizing how depressed and anxious she was without Jess. She had pacified both the doctor and Molly by assuring them that she had written to Jess, that he would be meeting her at the station, and that she would go directly to bed and stay there for the duration. She had reasoned with Molly that she'd be no help at all in closing up the house at West Point and attending to the other last-minute details that had to be finalized before their move.

She smiled to herself now as she thought of Molly bustling around in furious fashion; the practical-minded housekeeper considered wasting time to be a most grievous sin. If Kerry knew Molly, she'd be arriving in Washington within a day or two at the most.

Her thoughts returned to Jess, and her eyes danced with fond amusement as she imagined his surprise when he saw how round she'd grown in only three weeks. He had been in Washington for some months now, getting his ministry established and coming home to her when he could manage the time. With Molly's help she had managed affairs at West Point, preparing for the move and waiting—none too patiently—for the parsonage repairs to be completed so she could join Jess in their new home.

Now it had been three weeks—an eternity—since she had been with him. Wringing her hands together impatiently, she glowed with the thought that soon she could once more bury her head in the safe, warm haven of her husband's strong shoulder. They would talk about his new pastorate, the "weesy one," as Molly referred to their unborn child, and all that had happened since they'd been apart. Everything would be lovely.

For now, though, she must get on with her tour of the house. Afterwards, she would rest so she'd be fresh and clearheaded for the reunion with Jess.

Gathering her long skirts just above her ankles, Kerry left the parlor, stopping only once to glance behind her before making her way to the kitchen.

"Sure, and I hope all the rooms aren't as cold and unfriendly as that parlor," she mumbled to herself.

The dining room, however, did nothing to reassure her. It was damp and drearily formal, with its enormous mahogany table and chairs and heavy, gray drapes. The large, elaborately carved fireplace gave the room its only semblance of warmth.

Shuddering with dismay, Kerry entered the kitchen expecting the worst. But the large, comfortable room evoked a sigh of relief; it was far more welcoming and cheerful than she'd anticipated. In front of a wide, brightly curtained window, sat a child's replica of the long pine table and chairs that occupied most of the center area of the room. All the furniture, including the massive corner cupboard, appeared to be plainly and sturdily constructed and well used.

Perhaps I'll just stay in here until Jess arrives, she thought to herself, knowing full well that her inquisitive nature would allow her to do no such thing. She decided to explore no further downstairs but to have a look at the second floor. After peering up the dark flight of steps leading off the kitchen, she immediately returned to the reception hall to use the front stairway.

By the time she reached the landing of the second floor, Kerry was breathless and had to stop to rest. After a moment, she moved slowly down the dim, narrow hall, stopping to open the first door on her left. When it revealed only a small linen closet she went on. The next door opened onto what was obviously the master bedroom.

Sure, and Molly will be calling this place the "house of shadows," she thought with a grim smile. She held onto the door frame for a moment to ease the shortness of breath. Glancing around the room with a critical eye, she decided that the former occupants, devoted servants of the Lord though they might have been, must have also been of sour and dolorous natures. The room was as dark and intimidating as the parlor. An enormous bed with a towering headboard dominated the entire room; its wood was so dark as to be almost black. The dressing table was

13

massive and looked like a museum piece. Only a big, sturdy-looking rocking chair close to the fireplace cheered her spirits. At least the room wasn't totally bereft of human comforts.

Ah, well, Jess always said that Molly could work her domestic magic with even the most miserable of dwellings. Certainly the gloomy parsonage would offer a challenge.

She suddenly felt a terrible longing for the staunch Irish house-keeper. Molly had readily and willingly taken Kerry under her wing when, as the reluctant ward of Jess Dalton, the Academy chaplain, she had arrived at West Point three years ago. She had grown to love Molly as much as she thought she would have loved her own mother, had she ever known her.

Hesitantly, she walked the rest of the way into the bedroom. She knew her imagination must be playing tricks on her, but once more she was overwhelmed by an oppressive sense of something not quite right about the house. It felt especially strong in this room.

Kerry wondered if carrying a child would give a woman these peculiar sensations. But wouldn't Molly have told her so if that were the case? Sure, and she'd appointed herself as Kerry's advisor in all other matters, even to sitting her down and giving advice to the bride on the eve of her wedding day.

She thought then of Jess and smiled longingly—her dear, beloved Jess. He had been certain that the fourteen years' difference in their ages would prohibit her from loving him, when in truth she had loved him almost from the day she first arrived at West Point. He was a mountain of a man, both physically and spiritually. She missed him to the point of grief when they were apart. But he'd soon be gathering her into his embrace again, and all these silly fears would vanish.

So determined was she to banish as much of her uneasiness as possible, Kerry nearly managed to ignore the slightly swaying shadow beside the chest of drawers in the corner. When it moved again, she straightened her shoulders and thrust out her chin—though she could feel her lower lip trembling. Walking stiffly and determinedly in the direction of the subtle movement, she felt all the while the forbidding darkness closing in on her.

Jess had often said that fear was the hammer of Satan; well, she wouldn't be allowing Satan to pound at her with that or any other of his tools. She would face squarely on whatever was moving there in the corner.

Her resolve weakened somewhat when she saw the shadow weave ever so slightly to the right, then back to the left. Reflections from the outside, no doubt. Still, Kerry's mouth went dry and her breath caught in the tightness of her throat. She wiped her hands uncertainly on the skirt of her dress, wanting very much to bolt from the room and run from the house. But she kept walking.

In the silence of the room, she could hear the rapid pounding of her heart. Then, she met her terror face to face . . . or rather, face to form. There in the dark swayed a dress form, dimmed and brightened by ebbing shadows from a slightly open window.

Framing her face with her hands and weak with relief, she laughed at her own foolishness. "Ah, Kerry O'Neill Dalton, to think that you'll be having a child of your own one day soon, when if the truth be told, you're still a fanciful child yourself!"

Her feelings of foreboding now discharged, she whispered a brief, fervent prayer of thanks and started toward the rocking chair for a moment's rest. Smiling to herself as she glanced again at the dressmaker's form that had caused her panic, she stated merrily, "I'll not be telling my Jess what a silly lass his wife is. Sure, and we wouldn't want him to be having second—"

Her words were cut off by an unexpected roar of thunder which muffled her blood-chilling scream of terror as two burly arms imprisoned her. A crashing blow to her head sent her reeling to the floor.

A hulking shape crouched over Kerry's unconscious form. Her assailant gagged her and tied her hands behind her back with a piece of rough rope. Then he pushed and shoved her body into a bulky burlap sack and carried her clumsily down the stairs to a waiting carriage in the back of the house.

CHAPTER TWO

K erry awoke in pain to a darkness streaked with angry, frightening colors. She felt a sudden, hard jolt to her body, as if someone had kicked her down a flight of stairs. Weak and disoriented, she struggled to fight her way to consciousness.

The darkness engulfing her was more stifling than the gag that had been stuffed into her mouth to choke her screams of fear and rage. She gathered her wits enough to realize that she was trapped in some sort of covering. She couldn't move her hands, bound as they were behind her back. Worst of all was the way her body was bent, nearly doubled and crammed into an incredibly small space. She felt bruised and shaken, as if she'd been punched over and over again.

Tears of panic scalded her eyes and ran unchecked down her face, collecting in the rag that had been cruelly stuffed into her mouth and fastened tightly behind her head. She tried to scream for help, but the gag kept her from making a sound. She tried to pray but was too stricken with fear to do more than cry silently for the Lord to rescue her. She needed Jess, desperately craved

17

his presence, his strength. She needed Molly, her indomitable spirit, her unshakable courage.

But there was no one, no one but an unseen, unknown captor. She was totally alone—alone in the darkness with her fears, her soundless prayer, and her unborn child.

Oh, Father, help me. Help my babe. Please, Lord, protect my babe.

A sudden thrill of relief suged through her when she felt something slide away from her head. Whatever she'd been trapped in was being removed. Large calloused hands pulled her free of what seemed to be a formless burlap bag. She was being rescued! Someone had found her!

But one glance at the face hovering inches from her own dispelled any hope she might have had for freedom. The man's head was large and oddly swollen. His wide-set eyes were pale and sullenly vacant of expression. His nose leaned to one side, giving the appearance of having been broken several times. Scar-layered skin stretched tightly over his blotched face, and he was completely bald. The man's misshapen skull had obviously been badly burned at some time in the past.

Kerry had seen more than her share of horrors among the destitute squatters in Ireland. More than once she'd tended the infants of starving, half-dead mothers, infants born with hideous deformities. She had prepared bloated, blackened bodies for burial when she was no more than a child herself, and she'd looked death in its ugly face all the way across the sea in the coffin ship that had brought them to America. But never before had she seen a human being so miserably deformed. Had she not been so totally terrified of the man and her situation, she would have felt an instant wave of pity for him. As it was, she could only stare at him, wide-eyed with fear.

He said nothing, but continued to remove the burlap covering from around her. Kerry looked at him with a pleading stare, waiting for him to remove the gag from her mouth. But he left it in place. She felt a torrent of nausea crash against her; for an instant she was certain she would faint. When the man stretched out his enormous hand to touch her face, she recoiled as if he'd slapped her.

He cocked his head and stared stupidly at her. Finally, he

removed the gag but immediately covered her mouth with his hand for another moment.

"Keep quiet," he ordered. He slowly removed his hand from her mouth as if testing her obedience.

"Wh—who are you?" Her voice was no more than a fragile thread of terror.

He gave her an angry, disapproving frown and shook his head vigorously as he untied her hands. "I said don't talk."

His voice was thick and deep. The effort those few words seemed to require of him, plus the empty, fixed stare of his eyes, alerted Kerry that he was dimwitted at best. Even in the throes of panic, her protective instincts for herself and her unborn child asserted themselves; her quick mind began to spin with a number of possible escape routes.

Her captor sat on his haunches and watched her quietly for a moment, then hauled himself clumsily to his feet and took a few steps away from her.

Kerry glanced quickly and uneasily about her surroundings. Her mind was darting too erratically to assimilate everything, but she knew she was in a basement. It was cool, dark, and smelled of mildew, dust, and grime. The only light was a gray ribbon from a small, dirty window high on the wall against which her captor was leaning.

The floor was unbelievably filthy; she instinctively grimaced with distaste when she saw the grime clinging to her dress. Her gaze moved furtively to the rotting wooden steps that led straight up. She couldn't see to the top; it was too dark. Her heart pumped a bit faster as she considered her chances.

The hulking man propped against the dirty block wall seemed only half aware of her presence. A large rat had caught his attention. The frightened creature squirmed under the heel of the man's heavy boot, twisting and squealing in a futile attempt to break free. Kerry watched the despised rodent with horror, cringing at its plight, so similar to her own.

She took advantage of the brute's preoccupation by appraising her surroundings thoroughly, trying to ignore the frequent cramping in her abdomen. Again, her glance went to the stairs, then to the corner beneath them where a large shovel rested. She looked from the shovel to the man, who had now stooped down to study his prey more closely. Only a few feet lay between him and the shovel.

Kerry drew in a deep, steadying breath and turned a determined, fierce glare at the man. "I demand to know why you've brought me here! You've hurt me, you know!"

He lifted his head and stared at her with dull indifference. "For the chief. You be quiet."

"What chief? What do you want with me?" Kerry cried.

He scowled at her for a long moment, and she wondered if she should have held her silence. Then, as if he hadn't heard her, the man returned his attention to the rat.

Kerry chewed her lower lip, then decided she had nothing to lose. "Why don't you put it in the bucket if you want to play with it?"

He looked up at her, puzzled.

"The rat," she said, glancing down at the creature beneath his boot. "You're going to lose it if you don't put it in something. There's a bucket over there by the window."

He studied her for a long moment, then turned slowly to scan the wall behind him, keeping his one foot steady and heavy on the rat. Kerry knew she had to act quickly but felt an instant of paralyzing uncertainty. Feeling her heart stop, she drew in a deep gulp of air and dashed to the corner beneath the steps. She grabbed the shovel.

He heard her movement, but his awkward position threw him just enough off balance to make him clumsy. Before he could react, Kerry lunged straight at him with the shovel raised high above her head.

He roared and made a dive for her legs, but he was too big and too slow. Though stiff from her previous confinement and somewhat awkward with the child she carried, Kerry was small and fast—and desperate. She came at her captor like a wild animal and brought the shovel down on his head with all her strength. He fell, landing flat on his face. Kerry heard a sickening thud as his head hit the floor.

She hoisted her skirts, raced up the stairs, and yanked furiously at the chipped doorknob until the swollen door finally gave way. Taking no thought of her surroundings, Kerry ran through an empty pantry and an airless, foul-smelling kitchen. Ahead of her she spied a dirty white door with broken panes of glass. She nearly tripped in her haste to reach it, mumbling a prayer of thanks when she found it unlocked. Flinging it open, she bolted outside and fled down sagging wooden steps into a yard littered with garbage and debris.

She halted only long enough to look around in panic, trying to gain a sense of direction. After a moment, she took off running toward what appeared to be a road behind a dilapidated carriage house at the rear of the lot.

Screaming, she raced into a street thick with mud from an earlier rainstorm. The mire sucked at her shoes and held her back. Crazed with fear, Kerry stopped long enough to pull the shoes from her feet and fling them aside before resuming her flight.

She was vaguely aware of sagging frame buildings and the smell of decay. She almost ran into an abandoned cart, slipped, regained her balance, and went on. Hot tears of panic blinded her as she ran, and the brief, sharp cramps she'd experienced earlier intensified to fierce spasms that nearly stopped her getaway. But she continued to run, crying and screaming Jess's name. She ran as though death itself were chasing her until one huge crushing wave of pain brought her down, hurling her to her knees in the mud. A blanket of terrifying darkness closed in. She cried for Jess once more, then surrendered to the yawning whirlpool of oblivion.

CHAPTER THREE

Jess was impatient. He wouldn't have stopped by his office at the church at all if Charles Payne, his secretary, hadn't accompanied him and the White family to Baltimore. Upon their return, Charles needed to stop by the office to get his carriage.

Jess had declined his secretary's offer to drop him at home. Thanks to his years of daily crossing the grounds at West Point, walking was as natural to him as breathing. He could cover the short distance from the church to the parsonage on Lafayette Square in only moments.

It was nearly dusk by the time he approached the parsonage. His heart began to thud heavily with anticipation. How he had missed his beloved Kerry! Only three weeks parted, but it felt more like three years. His days had been somber and meaningless without her smile; the nights had seemed endless.

If ever a man loved a woman to the point of desperation, certainly his love for Kerry bordered on it. These past three weeks had taught him how utterly dismal and empty his life would be without her. His waking hours were filled with the memory of

23

her dancing emerald eyes, the dimpled smile that could sparkle mischief as readily as affection, and the softly curling riot of copper hair that never failed to fascinate him. His dreams were filled with a love so passionately intense, yet so tenderly sweet, that he sometimes struggled with feelings of guilt.

He had promised his Lord and himself, when he'd first accepted the call to the ministry, the nothing would ever take precedence in his heart over his servanthood to Christ. While he believed with all his heart that his and Kerry's love was God-ordained, a priceless gift from their creator, the depth of his love for her occasionally frightened him. At those times, he would have to force himself to surrender even this, his heart's devotion to this small, fiery wisp of a girl, and ask his Lord to keep that love from becoming an obsession.

At this particular moment, attempts to bring his excitement under control were in vain. He was practically running, craning his neck for a glimpse of the stately brick parsonage which sat a respectable distance back from the street.

She should have arrived hours ago. Would she be fretful that he hadn't met her at the station as he'd promised? Ah, well, he'd rid her of her peevishness in short order. His smile transformed his care-lined face into a younger countenance. He was dusty and hot and rumpled. His curly mane of black and silver hair badly needed brushing; even his beard bore the evidence of a harried journey on a hot August day. But more than anything else, he was a man aglow as he raced those last few feet to the walkway of his house.

He stopped, puzzled, when he saw an unfamiliar buggy tied in front. Entering the gate, he saw that the front door was open, and Mackenzie was standing just outside it on the porch, turning his head this way and that as if watching for someone.

Jess glanced once more over his shoulder at the buggy, then back to the caretaker as he made quick work of the remaining few steps to the porch.

"Mack?" He nodded to the big, stern-faced Irishman. "What are you about so late in the day? Have you just arrived with my wife?" He peered hopefully inside the door.

Jess stared with surprise as the burly caretaker raised a large, calloused hand to block his entrance. The deep frown of concern on Mackenzie's face triggered a sudden sense of impending disaster.

"What is it, Mack?"

"Pastor, it's bad trouble you have, I fear," the big man muttered grimly.

"Trouble?" Jess suddenly found it difficult to breathe. "What kind of trouble? Kerry?"

Mackenzie heaved a sigh of regret. "She's been put to bed, sir. She's upstairs, and she'll be all right. But you've trouble all the same." Jess stared at him, unwilling to discover what awaited him inside the house. He had a sudden, irrational desire to delay the encounter as long as possible, but a sharp stab of fear quickly overcame his hesitancy.

"Kerry—" He hurled himself through the door and took the stairs two and three at a time.

Adeline Corbett, his widowed neighbor, stood at the top of the staircase talking with a man Jess instantly recognized: George Marshall, a member of his congregation, a physician, and undoubtedly the owner of the buggy outside. They turned to Jess; he nearly stopped dead on the stairs when he saw the pained expressions on their faces.

Reaching the landing, he looked from one to the other with a growing sense of dread. "What is it? What's happened?"

Mrs. Corbett touched his arm uncertainly. Her usually flawless coiffure was in disarray, her clear blue eyes kind and concerned. "Mr. Dalton—"

By now, Jess was frantic beyond civility. "Where is she? What's wrong?"

"Pastor, please don't go in there just yet," the doctor said firmly, inclining his head toward the closed bedroom door. "Your wife has had a terrible experience, and there are a few things you need to know before you see her."

A wave of impatience washed over Jess, followed by raw fear. "What are you talking about? Is she ill?"

Dr. Marshall placed a strong, restraining hand on Jess's elbow. "Mr. Dalton, listen to me. Apparently your wife was—abducted. She's been injured. I've given her laudanum to make her more comfortable and to calm her."

"Abducted!" Jess wrested himself out of Dr. Marshall's grasp and moved toward the door of the bedroom, but the doctor stopped him again, this time with a sharp command.

"Pastor!" He immediately softened his tone when he saw the stricken look of disbelief on Jess's face. "Mrs. Dalton is all right. But I'm afraid . . ." His voice drifted off, and he shifted his gaze away from the intense emotion he saw in Jess's eyes.

The baby?" Jess mumbled hoarsely.

Dr. Marshall shook his head. "I'm so sorry. I couldn't save the child."

"Our baby is—dead?" Jess repeated in a hoarse whisper.

Again the doctor nodded. "I tried everything I know, Pastor, believe me. But your wife was badly hurt. She appears to have been pushed or dropped from a considerable height, perhaps a flight of stairs."

He spoke hurriedly, tapping one wrist with a white envelope that he was holding in the other hand. "Somehow she got away. Apparently, she ran until she passed out. She must not have been all that far away because she got within a few houses of the parsonage. One of your neighbors saw her from a window and went to help. She said Mrs. Dalton was calling your name before she fainted. The lady who found her screamed for help, and Mackenzie heard her from his cottage. He carried your wife out of the street, then came for me."

Jess shook his head back and forth in stunned confusion. "Abducted? Who would do such a thing to her?" He turned anxious, hurting eyes toward Mrs. Corbett. "Does Kerry—does my wife know about the baby?"

The silver-haired woman's eyes filled with tears. "Oh, Mr. Dalton, I'm so sorry. Yes, she knows."

"What she doesn't know, yet," the doctor interrupted hesitantly, clearing his throat, "is just as bad, I'm afraid."

The big pastor towered over the small, sandy-haired doctor. Jess was a man accustomed to having people turn in the street and take a second look at him because of his uncommon stature and a powerful physique. Yet, at this instant, he felt much like a small boy, a small frightened boy who knew he was about to hear something dreadful, something that would alter his entire life.

"Mr. Dalton," the doctor glanced uneasily at Adeline Corbett, who turned away and walked down the hall to give them privacy. He laid his hand on Jess's coat sleeve in a gesture of comfort. "Pastor, I'm terribly sorry, but Mrs. Dalton—well, there can be no other children. She was so badly injured . . ." He left his sentence unfinished.

Jess had known words could wound; he had felt their stab of agony more than once in his life. He had seen others reel beneath the assault of words that spoke of incurable illness, the passing of a loved one, or the destruction of something that had taken a lifetime to build. He knew the power of words to open or crush the heart.

Yet, all his years of experience as a minister, chaplain, and counselor hadn't prepared him for the pain that now slashed through his soul at the doctor's announcement. His grief wasn't only for himself; it was more for Kerry. With an aching heart, he knew what this would do to his beloved, the burden of sorrow it would place upon her spirit.

He swallowed once, then again with great difficulty. Meeting the doctor's gaze, he asked, "You're certain?"

George Marshall nodded sadly. "I'm sorry, Pastor, truly I am.". He drew a deep breath, then said more firmly, "I wouldn't want to minimize your wife's condition. She's suffered major internal injuries and severe hemorrhaging. Actually, she should be hospitalized, but I'm reluctant to move her. Mrs. Corbett mentioned a housekeeper. Will she be available to help care for Mrs. Dalton?"

Jess rubbed the back of one hand over his eyes and tried to grab onto at least a thread of reason. His voice was tremulous and uncertain. "Molly—yes. She should be here within the next few days."

"Good. I'm sure Mrs. Corbett and some of the other women in the church will help until then." He hesitated for an instant, glancing down at the envelope in his hand. "Pastor, this was brought to the house no more than a few moments after I arrived to tend to your wife." He handed the envelope to Jess. "Mackenzie said a Negro child delivered it saying a gentleman had given

27

it to him with the instruction that you were to read it right away."

Bewildered, Jess ripped open the message and began to read, stiffening with shock as he scanned the words. His chest tightened, and an excruciating pain assaulted his head. He felt the hot taste of nausea well up in his throat, and for an instant he nearly staggered. The note had been scrawled in large, childlike print: You can have the woman back if you agree to take her and your abolitionist garbage back to the North where you belong. There's no room for you in this city. You'll be contacted in a few hours for your answer.

He dangled the note from trembling fingers for a moment, then extended it to the doctor. He read it quickly, glowering with angry indignation.

"They wrote this not knowing she got away," he said tightly, glancing up at Jess. "As I said, it came only moments after I arrived."

Jess clenched his hands into rigid fists, fighting to put down the lashing waves of rage and fear roaring through him. Something deep inside him felt as if it were about to explode and shatter his sanity, but he knew he had to hold himself together for Kerry's sake.

He started to speak but the words choked in his throat. Putting out a hand to steady himself on the domed newel post of the stairway, he pulled in a deep breath and said in a ragged, pain-dulled voice, "Doctor, could you please—would you do just two things for me?"

"Anything I can, Pastor," the doctor answered quickly.

"Would you call the authorities and ask them to come? Then get a message to General Cummins for me. Ask him if he'll have Molly Larkin, my housekeeper, contacted at West Point. Tell her she's to leave there immediately. Kerry needs her."

"I'll see to it right away. And I'll return in a few hours to check on Mrs. Dalton."

Jess's mouth was now set in a hard, determined line. "Now, I've got to see my wife. Please!"

"Of course. But she may not be aware that you're with her, Pastor. If she does wake up, you mustn't let her become agitated again. She's already far too weak."

Jess nodded, taking an unsteady step toward the bedroom door. He hesitated and turned back to Dr. Marshall. "Doctor, the baby . . ."

The small, sad-faced doctor met his gaze with understanding. "A boy."

Jess looked away from him toward the wall, the stairway, then to Adeline Corbett. He nodded, a gesture of terrible, helpless grief. A son; he had had a son. "Where is he?"

"Everything has been taken care of, Pastor," the doctor replied gently. "We'll discuss arrangements later after you've had some time with your wife."

Jess turned away and walked to the closed door of the bedroom. He stopped for only an instant, drew in another long, unsteady breath, and lifted his shoulders. *Help me bear this, Father. Help me endure this for her—to be strong—for her.*

With only her pale oval face visible from beneath the lightweight blanket, Kerry looked like a child. Two unhealthy circles of red darkened her cheeks. Otherwise, she was white and drawn, her profile oddly serene. Her eyes were closed, and her breathing was shallow but even. A faint suggestion of pain hovered about her mouth.

The rocking chair he had bought especially for her sat near the bed, and Jess now moved it even closer. Not taking his eyes from Kerry's face, he quietly removed his black suit coat and laid it gently on the foot of the bed. He sank into the rocker and reached for her hand.

She stirred slightly but didn't awaken. He felt strangely relieved, as yet unwilling or unable to face her pain. What would he say to her? What could he say to her? How was he to tell her that the dream she had cherished since the early days of their engagement—and every day since—had been brutally destroyed by some unknown maniac?

I'm going to give you a house full of sons, my Jess, fine, strong sons to carry on the tradition of yourself and all the other Dalton men. We'll have us a hearth and home filled with big, curly headed sons who will idolize their father, as they should.

She had been so impressed—too impressed, he'd sometimes feared—with the generations of Dalton men who had spent their lives working to improve the lot of others, like his lawyer-father

29

and politician-grandfather. She had promised him that together they would continue the line. He had teased her that he'd also like a little girl or two "with copper curls and shamrock eyes like their mother." His eyes burned with unshed tears when he remembered the way she had told him about their baby. She had been so impatient to begin their family. When two years passed without a child, she had begun to worry. More than once she had cried out her fears on his shoulder.

But then came the evening when he arrived at the house to find the dining room looking like something out of one of the currently popular romantic plays. The best silver and china gleamed on the lace-covered table, and the room was aglow with candlelight. Kerry, wearing her deep green velvet evening gown—his favorite—looked mysterious and excited.

Her intention, she disclosed later in the evening, had been to say absolutely nothing until after dinner. But as soon as he walked into the dining room and lifted a questioning brow at the lavish table, she began to bounce from one foot to the other and wring her hands together, as she often did when she was excited. Her carefully designed strategy immediately crumbled, and she gave way to a peal of nervous laughter and a tumble of words announcing the expected event. She'd been upset with herself for hours afterward because she hadn't been able to carry off her original scenario.

Now, he leaned close to her, holding her hand and studying her slender fingers with great sadness. His eyes brimmed with tenderness and an unfathomable depth of love never seen by anyone except the young woman lying next to him.

For one bittersweet instant, he saw her again as she had appeared to him just three years past, a child-woman in a faded gingham dress and a worn black cloak. She had stepped reluctantly off the steamer at West Point, defensively clutching her small shabby valise to her side. She had been eighteen years old that bright autumn day when the defiant lift of her chin and sparkling emeralds in her eyes had gone straight to his heart and impaled him. His love had belonged to her from that moment on, though he had fought against if for months because of the vast age difference between them—and because he was, after all, supposed to be her guardian and protector.

Memories—such a wealth of memories flooded his heart as he brought her hand to his lips and held it there in a need to be as close to her as possible. His heart ached with silent words of self-recrimination and regret.

Ah, Kerry . . . mavournee,* what have I brought you to? I've torn you away from the only real security of your life. We had so much—a home you'd grown to love, a happy life together—and I asked you to leave it all for—this?

He tried to pray and instantly felt the arid desolation of his soul. He had to force the words from his heart in an anguished whisper.

I thought you called me here, Lord. I was so sure it was your will and not my own. But is this what you have called me to, this monstrous, terrifying nightmare? Why . . . why would you allow this to happen to us—to this little girl who loves you so totally, so innocently? Have you brought us to this place only to break our hearts and wreck our lives? Why, Lord—why?

He shook his head in an attempt to throw off his questioning and doubt. Even now, in the midst of this unexpected sorrow, his faith and his love for his Lord had to be greater than doubt, larger than confusion.

Still, hadn't he already questioned the wisdom of leaving West Point? It had taken only days for him to discover that a strong element of hostile opposition to him was present within this new congregation. His reputation had preceded his arrival, largely because of the books and newspaper articles he'd written over the years dealing with the sin of slavery, the child labor problem, the degrading labor conditions in the factories, and the oppression and abuse of those thousands of immigrants now crowding the shores of the country.

He had discerned that for every person who wanted him here and agreed with his views on equality under God, there were three others who violently opposed him, both as a minister and as a man. Many of these were politicians of great influence and power; the influential southern senator John Calhoun was one of them.

Yet in spite of the obvious difficulties facing him, when he prayed for direction, his spirit sensed God's instruction to stay.

But now? Kerry abducted, their child dead, all hope of future children lost to them—and the threat of further violence implicit in the note. Would the abductors try again once they learned of her escape?

Suddenly Kerry stirred, moving her head on the pillow with a moan of protest. The fingers of her free hand fluttered lightly upon the blanket. Her eyes opened slowly, then blinked. For a moment, she stared into Jess's face with no recognition. But as he watched, he saw gradual, unwilling recollection dawn in her gaze, mirroring his own anguish and deepening to a bottomless despair.

"Jess, oh, Jess . . ." She tried to raise herself to him, her arms reaching out to him, but he quickly restrained her, moving from the chair to the edge of the bed and gathering her gently into the circle of his arms.

He held her tenderly but securely. "Please, love, lie still. You must be very quiet for now," he murmured, pressing his lips softly against her temple.

But she wouldn't listen. She raised herself to rest her head in the hollow of his shoulder.

"No, love, don't." He felt her slender body begin to heave beneath his hands, and he thought his heart would shatter with the combined weight of their shared grief.

"Our babe—oh, Jess, our babe—"

His shirt was quickly wet with her tears, and the russet waves of her hair grew damp with his own. He groped for control, but her pain was more than he could bear.

"I know, I know, love, but you're all right, and how I thank the merciful Lord for that."

She sobbed even harder against him. "A son, Jess. I had a son for you . . . our son . . . and I never . . . even saw . . . his face."

He clung to her as though he could somehow infuse her with his own strength, unstable as it was at the moment. "Kerry, darling . . . don't . . . please. You'll hurt yourself."

"He never drew a breath, Jess not even a breath . . ."

"Shh . . . I know, I know. But God needs little ones in his heaven, too, love, not just older souls."

"They wouldn't let me see him . . ."

"Yes, love, I know. But it's best that you didn't." He tried, tried with all his being not to give in to his own sorrow, but he simply couldn't control the knifing grief any longer. He wept with her, not knowing whether he was agonizing more for the loss of his son or the pain of his wife. They clung to each other and mourned together and attempted to draw strength from each other.

Finally a long time later, Kerry was able to tell him what had happened. She described the man who had abducted her and conveyed as many details as she could remember about the house where she had been taken.

"If only I hadn't insisted on coming ahead without Molly," she sobbed. "If only I had't run, if I hadn't tried to get away. Perhaps our babe would have been all right, then . . ."

"Kerry—" Jess's voice was no more than a harsh whisper. "You must promise me that you'll never ever blame yourself for what happened! You did all you could—you tried to save our child— and yourself. The baby . . . the baby was most likely injured beyond help when you were . . . pushed down the stairs or whatever that monster did to you."

As if he suddenly realized he might be hurting her with his tight grasp, he relaxed his big hands and patted her reasurringly. "There's no explaining what happened today, love of my heart," he said softly. "Some things . . . we just aren't meant to under- stand . . . only accept."

He pushed a damp lock of hair behind her ear and kissed her forehead with infinite tenderness. "I've missed you so terribly, love."

Her voice caught on a choked sob. "Today was to have been such a happy time for us . . ."

"We'll still have our happy times, my darling," Jess attempted to soothe her. "We'll have to wait awhile for them, but we'll have them again, I promise you."

She pulled away from him enough to see his face and laid her hand gently upon his bearded cheek. "I'll have no happy times again, my Jess, until I give you a son."

Too late, he tried to stop the stricken look of dismay that

glazed his face. He knew she had seen and, with the unerringly acute insight so much a part of her nature, Kerry immediately sensed his anguish.

Her eyes studied him relentlessly, and a terrible fear began to settle over her features. "Jess?" Her always husky voice darkened even more.

He could do nothing but stare at her with helpless pain.

A slow-dawning, reluctant awareness filled her gaze. "Oh, no . . ." she breathed.

His heart wrenched at the awful expression on her lovely, ravaged face. "Kerry . . . love . . ."

"No . . . please . . . nooo . . ." The chilling sound of desolation pouring from her was the ancient, grief-stricken keen of the Irish mourner.

Jess wrapped her tightly against him as though to absorb her pain into himself. "My love . . . my love . . . I'm so sorry. . . ."

"Barren . . . am I barren, Jess?" she cried against him. "Please, no . . . not that . . . oh, please anything but that . . ."

All he could do was hold her against his aching heart. He had never felt so helpless in his life. There were no words; there was no comfort.

When Kerry finally realized he wasn't denying her protests, that her fear was an unbearable reality, she collapsed limply in his arms and gave way to a near irrational, helpless fit of weeping.

Jess continued to hold her and to make soft, soothing sounds of comfort as he tried to console her. But all the while, something dark that had been imprisoned deep inside him for the last hour banged angrily against his chest in hopeless fury, clamoring for release. A terrible, scalding rage threatened to cast aside the faith that had been a part of his life for as long as he could remember. Everything in his being cried out for revenge.

For years, he had believed himself to be a man of God, a servant. But at this moment of his life, he knew himself to be a man capable of blinding hatred. Someone should pay for what had been done to the shuddering, weeping girl in his arms. Someone must pay for destroying his beloved Kerry's dream, her hope . . . perhaps her very spirit.

CHAPTER FOUR

Kerry awoke feeling drugged and irritable. For the first time in days the deep rose-colored bedroom drapes had been fully opened to flood the room with late-morning sunshine.

The room was stuffy, and her head pounded unmercifully as she attempted to accustom her eyes to the light. She half-rose from the pillows and squinted; someone was standing off to one side of the window.

Propping herself up on one elbow, she shielded her eyes with her hand. "Molly!" With a weak, relieved breath, she fell back against the pillows. "Oh, Molly—I'm so glad you're here." Her voice was no more than a broken whisper.

The tall, strapping housekeeper walked toward the bed. As usual, her silver braids were arranged in a perfect crown atop her head, and her sturdy, corseted body was encased in one of her immaculate white shirtwaists and a sensible brown skirt.

She came to stand beside the bed and folded her arms over her ample bosom. Gazing down at Kerry with unsmiling, maternal concern, she said lightly, "And so you've become a real slugabed, have you now?"

Kerry didn't answer, but simply looked up at the staunch Irish housekeeper with tear-clouded eyes. "When did you come, Molly?"

"Last night. I looked in on you as soon as I arrived, but you were sleeping too soundly to wake." She reached out and lay one plump hand gently on Kerry's forehead, smoothing a limp wisp of hair away from her face. "How are you feeling then, lass? You've had a bad time of it, I know."

Kerry turned her face away. "Oh, Molly . . . if only I hadn't been so determined to come ahead of you. If only I'd waited . . ."

Molly straightened and narrowed her eyes thoughtfully. "And didn't Dr. Green agree that you could come? You did what you thought best, lass, and you're not to be blaming yourself for things beyond your control."

Kerry turned to look at her, saying nothing for a long moment. When she finally spoke, her words were so soft Molly had to bend closer to hear. "I had a son, Molly . . . a little boy."

The housekeeper swallowed with difficulty, but her voice was steady. "Aye, lass, I know."

"I suppose Jess told you that—I can have no more children." Her eyes took on an unhealthy, burning glint. "I'm barren now."

Molly studied Kerry's face as she sat down on the bed beside her. "There's no denying you've been handed a sorrowful burden to carry, alannah.* But you'll not be bearing it alone, and that's God's truth. You have a husband who loves you more than anything and who needs you more than ten sons."

"No man needs a wife whose body is a desert," Kerry rasped bitterly.

Molly lifted her head a fraction, then said quietly, "Your body is for more than growing babes, Kerry Dalton. Above all else, you're to be a comfort and a haven for your husband."

"Jess deserves more than comfort. He's a man who should have children." Her eyes were smudged with dark shadows that only emphasized the glaring resentment of her gaze.

"And did he marry you, then, only for the sons you could give him?" Molly countered archly. "Faith, and I would have swore it was because the lad is totally possessed with love for you!"

Kerry tossed impatiently in the bed. "You don't understand!"

"And don't I now?" Molly challenged, abruptly softening her tone before she continued. "Have you thought I never wanted babes of my own? It wasn't Patrick who was at fault for our childless union."

The housekeeper's words silenced Kerry. She looked into Molly's kindly face with surprise. "But you were only married a short time before your husband died."

"Long enough to want his child more than anything," Molly said matter-of-factly. "Long enough to pray my heart empty night after night that the Lord would open my womb."

Immediately contrite, Kerry bit her lower lip and reached out to touch the housekeeper gently on her forearm. "I'm so sorry, Molly . . . I didn't know." She pushed herself up and rested heavily on both elbows. "Molly, tell me the truth. Does it still . . . cause you pain, that you have no children? There's such an awful hurting in my heart, Molly . . . I don't know how I'll ever live with it."

Molly glanced away for an instant. When she answered, her words came slowly and carefully. "Yes, lass, I know well the pain you're feeling. And I'll not be lying to you about it—there are times when the old hurting comes back to nag at my heart. It will haunt you now and again, too, no doubt."

She turned back to Kerry and looked directly into her eyes. "But you have a fine, wonderful man who loves you with all his being. That must be your consolation until our Lord sees fit to fill your life in other ways, to heal this hole in your heart. Don't you see, lass?" The housekeeper's voice grew intense. "Our Lord will not leave you empty of comfort forever."

Kerry wanted to believe her. She wanted desperately to believe that this pain now knifing her heart to shreds would eventually leave, that one morning soon she'd be able to face the day without cringing in the light of it. Yet, she couldn't help but wonder, as she turned her face away from Molly's compassionate gaze, if she would ever again feel anything but this agonizing, debilitating emptiness.

Molly rose from the bed. "I'll get some warm water so we can have us a bath now. Your hair is a fright, and your bed linen needs changing as well. Jess wanted to come in here early this morning already, but I told him he'd be waiting until I've had some time with you."

"Oh . . . don't let him see me like this, Molly! I must look terrible—I feel terrible."

"And hasn't the lad already seen you at your worst, now?" Molly said without gentling her words. "The widow woman next door—Mrs. Corbett, is it?—says he's barely left your side in three days going."

"Three days!" Kerry was stunned. "It's been . . . three days since . . ." The words died in her throat as she fell back onto the pillows.

"Aye, it has. The doctor has given you laudanum regularly, to ease things for you a bit. But our Jess has had to keep his wits about him, heartsore as he is, to help tend to you. Sure and he's had to push his grief aside for a time. But now it's for you to do your duty as a wife and be strong for him. He should not have to bear this alone any longer."

Molly's blunt words caused a flush of guilt to warm Kerry's cheeks. She was right, of course. The child had been as much a loss for Jess as for her. And he had gone through the worst of it alone. "I know you're right, Molly, but . . ." She left her thought unfinished and turned to stare bleakly at the wall.

"Listen to me, lass—" Molly's stern, no-nonsense tone made Kerry turn and face her.

The housekeeper's dark eyes held a mixture of concern and understanding. "Our Jess would not be the first strong, honorable man to be weakened or even worse by the trouble of one he loves."

Her next words, uttered with a low, level passion, chilled Kerry. "I have strong feelings about what has happened to the two of you, and I'm asking you to think on some things, for Jess's sake even more than your own. There's evil at work here, if I'm not sadly mistaken—an evil that's trying to put a stop to our Jess's ministry and influence. This thing that was done to you," she paused and drew in a deep, worrying sigh, "was done more to him, if you take my meaning."

When Kerry moved to prop herself up against the pillows, Molly bent to help her, then sat down on the edge of the bed again before continuing. "Our Lord has placed a few brave men in this world who are so fiercely strong, so unshakable in their stand for right, that there is seemingly no way for the devil and his henchmen to do them in."

She nodded to herself as if a thought had only now occurred to her. "Sure, and Jess is such a man," she said softly. In a stronger voice, she added, "What I'm thinking is that somebody has taken the measure of our Jess and knows his mettle, knows there is but one way to stop him."

The gaze she turned on Kerry was afire with anger and warning. "You're the way, lass. And it freezes my heart to think that someone else knows that. Jess's love for you is so great, so fierce—he draws strength and vigor and happiness from you, don't you see . . . it's a kind of weakness in a way, the only weakness in the man, to my eyes. What I fear," she stated darkly, "for you and for him, is that this . . . evil soul . . . is going to try to weaken—or even destroy—our Jess, using you as the weapon."

Kerry stared at her with incredulous, frightened eyes. "If you should be right," she questioned in a tremulous voice, "what can I do, Molly?"

The housekeeper seemed to consider her reply with great care, but her gaze never wavered. "What you need to do, I should think, is to be very strong. A bit stronger than they think you are," she said with a nod of her head and a strange little smile that quickly sobered. "A bit stronger . . . a bit braver . . . and a bit smarter."

They stared at each other in silence for a long time. Finally, Kerry lifted her chin just a fraction and said levelly, "I believe I'm feeling up to my bath now, Molly, if you'll help me. And—don't let Jess come in yet, please. I have it in my mind to surprise him by looking . . . stronger today."

The housekeeper nodded her approval. "Fine, lass. We'll give you a pretty nightdress to put on after your bath—we'll fix your hair a bit, too. Then, while you and Jess visit, I'll make some stirabout for your breakfast. We must get some strengthening food into you quickly." She clucked her tongue and shook her head. "I've not seen you so poorly since you first stepped off the steamer at the Academy."

39

"I remember what you called me that day, Molly," Kerry said, smiling for the first time since Molly had entered the room.

"And what was that, lass?"

"You said I was no more than a whisper in the wind," Kerry replied, her gaze distant with the memory.

Molly opened her mouth and started to answer, then stopped, studying the small, lithe girl under the blanket. "And I might have been right, you know," she said thoughtfully. "Sure, and it's a small thing, a wind's whisper, but it can't be stopped, don't you see? It can't be stopped at all."

She walked to the door, then turned back. With an evasive glance about the room, she cleared her throat and said awkwardly, "You're a fine lass, you know. And things will be all right for you and our Jess again, see if they're not." She then hurried out the door, closing it firmly behind her.

By the time Molly finished tending to her, Kerry was nearly faint with weakness. But she knew the effort had been worthwhile when Jess entered the room, stopping abruptly as an uncertain smile of relief broke across his face.

He looks exhausted, Kerry thought. A wave of tenderness for him flooded her, and she reached out to clutch his hand as he came quickly to her side. His eyes were deeply shadowed, and sharp lines of fatigue webbed across his face. She could tell he'd been raking his fingers through his unruly mane of hair, as he always did when he was worried or distraught. At the moment, he looked harried and slightly unkempt, but there was a definite glimmer of hope in his eyes as he took her hand, squeezed it gently, and bent to kiss her lightly on the forehead.

"You're looking infinitely better this morning, sweetheart." Kerry could hear the question in his voice.

"I'm feeling . . . much stronger, Jess. And so glad to know Molly is with us. Here," she patted the edge of the bed, "sit beside me."

He sank down gratefully onto the bed and studied her face. "It's so good to see you looking . . . more yourself, love," he said softly. "I've been so worried." His eyes drank in the clean lustre of her hair and the slight color to her cheeks. "Is it all right if I hold you?"

She opened her arms to him at once, and he immediately gathered her into a gentle, cautious embrace. "Oh, Kerry, beloved. How I've prayed that you'd be all right," he murmured into her hair. "I've been so frightened."

Kerry nestled her face against the soft white fabric of his shirt, allowing herself to draw comfort from his strength, as she had so many times in the past. "I don't want you to worry about me, Jess. I'll be all right, truly I will."

They remained that way for a long time, Jess holding her with extreme tenderness, smoothing her hair, rocking her gently back and forth as he would have a hurting child.

"I wish I could take you out of there and hold you properly—in our rocking chair," he said with a boyish smile.

Kerry glanced over at the massive rocker in front of the fireplace. "Is it our chair, then, Jess? I thought it was a part of the furnishings of the parsonage."

"No, I bought it for you," he explained, still smiling. "I thought since we were storing our furniture for now, it would be nice for you if you at least had a rocking chair of your own."

The gesture was so typical of him. Kerry felt her eyes mist. Always, his thoughts were of her—how to please her, how to make her happy, how to show his love for her. "Thank you, dearest. That gives me an incentive to get out of this bed as quickly as possible."

He gave her a small hug and smoothed her hair away from her forehead. "There are things we should talk about, if you're feeling well enough, love," he said quietly.

Kerry nodded. He released her gently from his embrace and helped her recline once more against the plump pillows, now smooth and fragrant with clean linen.

He told her of the note that had been received after her abduction and the futile investigation that had followed, revealing at the same time his belief that the abduction had been a way of striking at him. "The note leaves little doubt as to the motive behind the whole thing."

"There's no way of knowing who's responsible?"

He shook his head. "The authorities think they've found the house where you were taken. Your shoes were discovered near an abandoned area that's being considered for renewal; the street isn't too far from the Square, as a matter of fact. They searched for a number of places, and there's one with a basement that fits your description. But that's all they know. Nothing else."

"And you think they did all this to . . . drive you away, to make you leave Washington?" Kerry questioned him anxiously, remembering Molly's earlier words of warning.

A spark of anger glinted in his eyes. "That's how it would seem, yes."

Kerry felt the familiar weakness wash over her again. "Oh, Jess, how could anyone hate so much? I don't understand."

He clasped her hands in his and looked at her anxiously. "I'm tiring you. We'll not talk about this any more this morning."

"No! We must talk about it," she protested, trying to sit up but quickly falling back, too fatigued to make another effort.

"Kerry . . . please." He brushed her cheek with the fingertips of one hand. "All we can do is let the authorities handle this for now. For the next few weeks you won't be strong enough to leave the house anyway. In the meantime, I intend to make absolutely certain that you're not alone in the house at any time. We have to be extremely careful until . . . I decide what's to be done."

"To be done? What do you mean?"

He clenched his hands together in a gesture of agitation and glanced away from her. "I can't possibly stay here if there's any chance at all that they may try something like this again."

"Jess! You cannot leave! You were so sure the Lord was leading you when you agreed to come here. You can't simply give up." Could it be happening already, what Molly had spoken of? Was his fear for her beginning to chip away at the strength of his faith? "I won't let you do that," she stated firmly, clasping his shoulders with both hands.

Despair tugged at her heart when she saw the uncertain tormented expression in his gaze. "Kerry, they've already taken our son," he grated hoarsely. "And I might have lost you as well. Not for anything in the world will I stay here if you're in danger. We'll go back to the Academy—we'll live in the woods if we must. But I won't risk anything else happening to you."

42

"Oh, Jess," she said softly, only now coming to realize what an agony these past few days must have been for him. She drew his head down upon her breast and cradled him there, tenderly threading her fingers through his curly hair. "It will be all right, my treasure," she soothed. "You'll see. We're going to be all right."

He raised his head to look at her, and the depth of love and adoration in his gaze made her weak. "Yes, we will, love," he said softly. "As long as we're together, we'll be all right."

He stayed with her, holding her in his arms until she fell asleep. Even while she slept, he stayed, watching her, smiling softly at the way the copper waves of her hair tumbled stubbornly over her forehead. Occasionally, he would touch one finger lightly to her cheek or raise her hand to his lips and brush a tender kiss across her fingertips. Just before leaving her, he got to his knees beside the bed and prayed long and fervently from the depths of his aching, heavy soul.

. . . *Father, heal her heart. She's trying to be so strong, so brave—for me. But I know her too well and love her too much not to see the pain that's consuming her. Oh Lord, I can't pretend to know your ways or understand your will. At this moment, I admit that to my limited, human mind, there appears to be no balm for the wound inflicted upon my beloved's spirit, no possible way to fill the emptiness she's been left with. But if I've learned nothing else in the years I've walked with you, I've learned that you delight in doing impossible things for your children.*

So I ask you, Lord, in your time and in your will, to somehow give us a child. I'm pleading with you, Lord, not for myself—my beloved Kerry is enough for me; I don't need anything more than her love. But she so desperately wants a child, Lord. She wants that more than anything . . . and she has asked for so little in her life.

With you, there must be a way . . . oh, Father, in your love and in your mercy, make a way.

CHAPTER FIVE

A month later, Kerry sat in her rocking chair by the long, narrow bedroom window. Her slender fingers played idly at the light quilt over her lap as she gazed out the window, staring mindlessly in the direction of the White House. The day was damp and gloomy, and her disposition equally dismal as she remembered other September afternoons, cool but bright and cheerful with West Point sunshine.

She was bored and restless—too unsettled to concentrate on anything. No one would yet allow her to lift a hand about the house. She didn't know who was worse, Molly or Jess, when it came to treating her like an invalid, though it was true enough that she didn't feel overly strong. Nor was she likely to, she thought with a touch of frustration, if they continued to coddle her so.

They weren't fooling her. Jess was especially transparent, insisting that she mustn't so much as poke her nose outside the bedroom. The truth was that both he and Molly felt more comfortable about her safety as long as she was cooped up inside the house. Even Molly—usually impatient with idleness—was doing her part to keep Kerry tucked safely under her wing.

She turned toward the door, brightening somewhat when she recognized Mackenzie's slow, heavy footsteps on the stairs. She smiled, knowing the caretaker would pause at the bedroom door, clear his throat gruffly, and ask if he could enter.

Anticipating him, she called out, "Come in, Mackenzie."

The door creaked on its hinges as the big, burly man pushed it open. He glanced inside before entering the room, then greeted her as he always did, with a small nod of his balding head and a polite, "missus." In one hand he clutched his cap, while the other hand appeared to be holding something inside his woolen vest. Behind wire-rimmed spectacles, his dark gray eyes darted around the room.

"Is the housekeeper about?" he asked shortly.

Kerry sighed. While Jess seemed amused by the feud between Mackenzie and Molly, she was bewildered and troubled by it. Not only did she love Molly as a mother, but she had grown especially fond of the taciturn caretaker. The kindness Kerry had detected in his eyes at their first meeting had revealed itself further over the passing weeks as a very definite trait of the big Irishman's nature, although he seemed to make a point of concealing it. From the beginning, he had taken Kerry as his own private charge, determined to assume sole responsibility for her well-being and comfort.

"I believe Molly is downstairs, Mackenzie. Wasn't she in the kitchen when you came in?"

He still didn't smile, but did relax his guarded look somewhat. "I came through the cellar door."

"Whatever for?"

"Didn't want to bring her wrath down on me. Here, missus—I found this poor mite wandering around my cottage. I thought perhaps you'd care to have him."

With a cry of surprise, Kerry watched as he gently removed from inside his coat a light gray tabby kitten with dark gray stripes. The kitten had four white-socked feet and appeared to be slightly cross-eyed.

The caretaker shyly offered the furry bundle to Kerry, who reached out for it with undisguised delight. "What a wonderful surprise, Mackenzie!" She raised the kitten in both hands and held it slightly away from her face for inspection. "Oh, the poor wee thing is no more than mere bones! And doesn't he have a funny little face!"

Two frightened green eyes stared out, accompanied by one loud and indignant meow. Kerry cuddled the kitten against her, crooning to it and smiling up at Mackenzie, who looked extremely pleased with her reaction.

"I can't thank you enough, Mackenzie! But you'll have to help me take care of him for a bit, I fear. The doctor still won't let me go downstairs."

With a brief shake of his head in agreement, the caretaker replied, "I'll fix him a basket right here in your room, missus. And I'll stop by every now and then to take him out for his little business."

Kerry gingerly set the kitten on his feet so she could watch him explore. He immediately became a different creature. Asserting his territorial rights, he inspected the room, padded around the bed, charged suddenly beneath it, then out from under it with a dive at Kerry's feet.

She burst into merry laughter for the first time in weeks, and Mackenzie's eyes glowed with silent pleasure as he watched her.

At that moment, Molly came charging through the open door, wearing a fierce frown and wiping her hands briskly on her apron.

"What is it, lass? I heard you cry out all the way—"

Her black eyes narrowed with suspicious disapproval when she saw Mackenzie. "And what might you be doin' up here, man? What have you done to upset the lass?"

Before the caretaker could utter one of his low, surly replies, the kitten, apparently startled by the housekeeper's unexpected entrance, hurled himself directly at Molly's feet, tackling her ankles with determined fervor.

Molly yelped in surprise and immediately began to hop up and down, first on one foot then the other, in an attempt to shake off her small attacker. Kerry covered her mouth with her hands as she desperately fought to control a burst of laughter. One glance at Mackenzie made it even more difficult to hold a straight face, for he was positively beaming at Molly's plight—the very first time Kerry had ever seen the solemn caretaker so much as crack a smile.

"Ochone!* Faith, and what have you let into this house, old man?" Still bristling with surprised indignation, Molly began to wildly flap her apron at the poor kitten, who scampered to safety under the bed, cowering there to peep out with cautious detachment.

"It's only a small kitten, Molly," Kerry said, hoping to ward off another shindy between the housekeeper and the caretaker. "Mackenzie found the poor thing wandering about outside and brought him in to me. Isn't he sweet looking?"

"Sweet?" Molly stared at her young mistress as though she thought Kerry had lost her wits. "He's a wild thing, a scavenger! Cats are deceitful creatures, every last one of them, sneaking about with their evil eyes—"

Mackenzie crossed his arms over his chest, still grinning wickedly. "The wee thing could use some food while I'm fixing it a basket; the missus wants to keep it close to her here in the bedroom."

The housekeeper planted her hands firmly on her ample hips and eyeballed the Irishman. "We will have no cat in this house! Shedding its fur and making a stink—"

"Molly—I want the kitten," Kerry declared firmly. "I've already chosen a name for him."

With his gaze still on Molly's face in an expression of spiteful satisfaction, Mackenzie asked, "And what will you be calling your new pet, missus?"

"Brian," Kerry said firmly. "His name is Brian Boru."

Molly drew in a sharp, horrified breath. "Boru?" she repeated in a scandalized tone. "You'd name this—animal—after our warrior king? A—cat named for the bravest, strongest king who ever drew breath upon the soil of Ireland?"

"Brian will grow into his name," Kerry said confidently, smiling to herself at Molly's shocked expression. "He will be a cat worthy of the title, I'm sure, won't you, Brian Boru?"

As though he knew he'd been granted a pardon, the kitten crept a few inches out from under the bed, then scurried the rest of the way from his hiding place to leap into Kerry's lap.

"Madness!" Molly snarled. "I'll not be cleaning up its messes, I'll tell you that right now! The both of you can blame yourselves for bringing this green-eyed goblin under our roof! And it's sorry you'll be for it, just see if you're not."

Having learned some years earlier that Molly's indignant explosions were quickly over and forgotten, Kerry turned an innocent gaze on the housekeeper. "Molly, there's some yarn in my basket there by the bureau. Would you give me a small ball of it, please?"

"Yarn?" With a suspicious arch of an eyebrow, Molly halted her rampage.

"Yes. Kittens love to play with yarn, you know."

Snorting with disgust, Molly hesitated, then marched stiffly over to the sewing basket and selected the tiniest ball of yarn she could find. Chin up and eyes flashing, she handed the yarn to Kerry with a withering glare.

The kitten immediately grabbed for it, tumbling off Kerry's lap and unraveling the yarn all across the bedroom floor. Kerry and Mackenzie laughed at its antics, while Molly sputtered to herself and tried to pick up the snarled yarn without tripping over it.

That was how Jess found them when he appeared at the bedroom door. "Kerry? Can you receive company? Ah, good—you're up."

With a puzzled but pleased smile, he walked into the room followed by two elegantly dressed ladies of extremely dignified appearance.

"Whatever is going on in here?" he said, crossing the room to kiss Kerry lightly on the forehead. "How good it is to hear you laugh again, sweetheart."

He straightened and turned to the ladies who had accompanied him into the room, and who now stood waiting a few feet inside the door. The taller of the two stared with incredulous disdain at the untidy room. She touched one hand to her perfect silver coiffure and lifted an expressive eyebrow at the other woman who was shorter, rounder, and appeared, Kerry thought, far less formidable.

"I've brought visitors, dear," Jess said, seemingly unconcerned by all the confusion in his bedroom. "Kerry, this is Mrs. North-cote." The tall, stately matron nodded to Kerry with a frosty smile. "And Mrs. Pence." Both women approached Kerry as they were introduced.

"Mrs. Northcote is president of the Ladies Benevolence Society at the church," he explained to Kerry with a smile and what she thought might have been a mischievous glint in his eye.

Somewhat intimidated by the tall, regal woman in the impeccable gray suit, Kerry smiled at her and her more kindly faced companion. "It's very nice to meet you, I'm sure," she said quickly, fervently wishing at least for Jess's sake, that she had been a bit more—composed for her first meeting with these obviously important ladies.

Mrs. Northcote stepped close enough to offer Kerry a book and a small box of chocolates. "Mrs. Dalton, we thought you might enjoy a book of poetry . . ." She let her words fall off, marked by a definite question as she glanced from Kerry to Mackenzie, whose work clothing was anything but spotless and whose level stare held a suggestion of challenge.

Her contemptuous gaze moved to Molly. The red-faced house-keeper, in an effort to capture the roguish kitten, had instead managed to hopelessly entangle her feet in a maze of yarn. Growling furiously under her breath, Molly was making a futile attempt to escape her self-made trap. Finally, she turned a scalding, pointed look on Mackenzie, which he unabashedly ignored.

Mrs. Pence smiled nervously and coughed. "We're so sorry for your loss, Mrs. Dalton. We do hope you're feeling better."

Kerry returned her smile with an uncertain glance at Jess, who, rather than appearing perturbed by the scene, seemed mildly amused. As if he sensed her concern, he placed a steadying hand on her shoulder and gave it a light squeeze.

"I—yes, thank you," Kerry managed to say.

Mrs. Northcote glanced from Kerry to Mrs. Pence with a look that clearly said she saw no evidence of grief in the room. Looking down her long patrician nose, she appeared to sniff the air around her. "You have—a new pet, Mrs. Dalton?"

Kerry followed her gaze to the corner of the bedroom, where a disinterested Brian Boru was walking away, leaving behind him a rather substantial puddle.

"Oh, mercy," she mumbled softly.

Unbelievably, Jess chuckled. "Who's your new friend, Kerry?"

"Mackenzie brought him to me," she replied under her breath.

The caretaker grabbed a nearby newspaper and hurriedly began to clean up the puddle. As soon as he finished, he left the room carrying the small, disgraced offender in his arms.

"We'll have to teach him some manners, I think," said Jess easily. "But as long as he can make you look as well and happy as you do this afternoon, he has a home for himself."

He then favored the two women from the church with a dazzling smile. "Ladies," he continued equitably, "while my household isn't always quite so frenzied, I can't bring myself to apologize, not when I've found my wife looking more herself than she has for weeks. Perhaps you'll be generous enough to excuse our confusion this afternoon."

Oh, and isn't the man a charmer, Kerry thought with a touch of affectionate pride. Molly had said often enough that Jess could melt the heart of a stone, once he set his mind to it.

Apparently unaffected by his charm, however, Mrs. Northcote replied in a stiff, disapproving voice, "We understand perfectly, Pastor."

She turned her frosty gaze back to Kerry. "Do I understand that you're originially from Ireland, Mrs. Dalton?"

From behind her chair, Jess's hand once more tightened on Kerry's shoulder.

"Ah . . . yes. Yes, I am," Kerry replied. "As are Molly and Mackenzie."

"Of course. Isn't that nice for . . . all of you." The queenly matron then directed her attention to Jess. "Tell me, Pastor, are you of Celtic bloodlines also?"

Kerry turned to look up at Jess. Something flickered in his deep blue eyes, and Kerry was unable to tell whether it was amusement or irritation.

"Indeed I am, Mrs. Northcote, though I prefer to think of myself as simply an American. As Christians, we're every one of us brothers and sisters, are we not?"

Amusement, Kerry decided. He was definitely enjoying himself.

"Indeed." The formidable Mrs. Northcote curled her lips as if she had developed an offensive taste in her mouth. Turning briskly to Mrs. Pence, she announced, "Marian, we must be going now. We still have a delivery to make to the colored school, you know. Besides," she added dryly, "we musn't tire Mrs. Dalton."

"The colored school?" Kerry repeated curiously.

"Why, yes, Mrs. Dalton. Your husband has initiated a new benevolence program for the church. We're providing a number of textbooks to assist one of the Negro schools in the city." Mrs. Northcote turned a smile on Jess which stopped short of her eyes.

Matching her smile with a far more genuine one of his own, Jess replied guilelessly, "And I'm extremely gratified that you ladies are giving the program your personal attention."

"Yes, well—" Mrs. Northcote flicked her gaze from Jess to Mrs. Pence. "You're certainly engaging our congregation in a number of—novel—programs, Pastor. Hopefully, these new ventures won't dilute our traditional ministries," she said pointedly.

With a final arrogant glance about the room, Lydia Northcote announced firmly, "Marian, we must go now. Mrs. Dalton, may we extend a welcome to our city as well as our sincere wishes for your recovery." She nodded to Jess and turned to go, stepping carefully around the trail of yarn that now led from Molly to the center of the room.

Jess escorted the ladies downstairs and out of the house but returned as soon as they were gone.

Once Molly disentangled herself enough to leave the room, Kerry looked up at Jess with a small grimace of apology. "Oh, Jess, I'm so sorry. I wouldn't embarrass you for the world. If only I'd known they were coming—"

He laughed at her discomfort, then carefully scooped her up into his arms, taking her place in the chair as he pulled her onto his lap. "Mrs. Dalton," he said softly, smiling into her eyes, "you could never embarrass me. Believe me, love, the ladies will recover nicely."

"I wonder," Kerry muttered worriedly. "They most likely think you married a brainless bumpkin."

"I married," he said firmly, "the most beautiful jewel of Ireland

52

and the most wonderful girl in the world." He kissed her soundly on her pouting mouth, then traced the curve of her cheek with one finger. "How are you, love?" he asked softly. "How are you feeling?"

"Better. Truly, I am," she quickly insisted when she saw his skeptical look. "The doctor says I can go up and down stairs in a few more days and begin taking short walks as well."

Jess immediately knitted his heavy dark brows together in a worried frown. "Promise me you'll go very slowly, love. You must be careful."

"I will," she agreed. "But—oh, Jess, I simply must find something to do. I can't bear sitting around here, staring out the window any longer."

He hugged her closer and coaxed her head onto his shoulder. "Are you that unhappy, love?"

"If our child had lived—" She stopped for a moment, unable to go on.

Jess tightened his embrace. "I know. Oh, Kerry—I want so much to be . . . enough for you. But I understand how you feel, dear, really I do."

She tipped her head up to look into his face. "Jess, you are enough for me. You make my life wonderfully full. It's just that . . . now that I know there will be no children for us, I need to find a way to fill the hours—something to give my life some . . . purpose. Molly will never allow me to do very much around the house—you know how she is. I simply have to find a way to keep busy."

"But you do understand that you can't leave the house by yourself yet, don't you, Kerry? Even when you're stronger, we have to get some answers about the abduction before we can feel that you're safe again."

She pulled back from him and looked into his eyes. "Jess, it's been a month now. And there have been no other incidents, nor do we know any more than we did at the beginning. You can't keep me locked inside this house forever, you know."

"I don't intend to. But I also don't intend to take any chances with your safety. None," he emphasized firmly.

Hearing the stubborn resistance in his tone, Kerry uttered a resigned sigh. "Let's talk about something else for now. Tell me about this new project of yours, the Negro school Mrs. Northcote mentioned. I didn't realize there were schools for black children here in Washington."

"It's uncommon, that's true," he admitted, "but Washington has quite a large free Negro population, and they're doing their best to keep some schools going. I've been trying to get the city churches interested in providing textbooks, desks, and other necessary supplies."

"And?"

He cushioned her head in the hollow of his shoulder and rocked back and forth. "I've managed to get a great deal of solid support from some of them. But for those willing to help, there are many more who think I'm quite mad."

"What about teachers? How do they get teachers?"

"It's difficult," he said with a deep sigh. "There's one, though, who's particularly good at what she does. A young black woman from the North—Cely Johnson. She worked for a wealthy family who owned a gigantic industrial complex in Massachusetts. They became aware of her intelligence and saw to it that she got an education. Then they funded her first year here in Washington to work with the children at one of the schools. She's done a phenomenal job, but she needs help desperately."

Kerry's mind began churning out all kinds of bizarre thoughts. She was quiet for a time, thinking about the brave black woman and the job she had undertaken by herself.

"Are you tired, love?" Suddenly aware of her silence, Jess stopped the rocking motion of the chair and tipped her chin upward to study her face with concern. "Do you need to lie down?"

"Oh—no, no, Jess. I'm fine. I was just . . . thinking."

His gaze bathed her with affection as he pressed his lips gently against her temple. "And what are you thinking about, little missus?" he asked, borrowing Mackenzie's pet address for her.

"Jess . . . why couldn't I help . . . when I'm well again?"

"Help?" he repeated blankly.

"Couldn't I be of some use—to Cely Johnson, for example?"

Surprised, Jess drew back from her and searched her eyes.

"You mean at the school?"

She nodded vigorously. "Listen to me, please—don't say no until you hear me out." Her words tumbled out in an excited rush as she tried to convince him. "You've tutored me for years, Jess, and haven't you said that I've learned quickly and well?"

He nodded his agreement.

"Well, don't you see? I could share with these children all you've taught me. What good is all my learning if I keep it to myself?"

When he started to protest, she hushed him with a finger over his lips. "No, now, wait—please. You said this Cely Johnson is trying to manage alone? That's a terrible burden, surely. I could be a real help to her, couldn't I? Do you know her, Jess?"

"I've met her, yes, but—"

"Then you could introduce us. I could be a kind of assistant to her perhaps. Oh, Jess, don't you understand? If I can't have children of our own, at least I could help someone else's!"

She framed his bearded face between her hands and gazed into his eyes intently. "Don't you see, Jess? It would give me a purpose—something important to do. I know I couldn't be a real teacher, but surely I could be of some value as a helper."

He searched her beloved face for a long moment. "The school is in a rough part of the city, Kerry—"

She pursed her lips thoughtfully. Finally, her eyes brightened. "Perhaps Mackenzie would be willing to take me back and forth in the carriage?"

Jess gently combed her hair with the fingers of one hand. "I believe Mackenzie would take you to China and back if you asked. The poor man cherishes every hair on your head." He smiled softly at her. "But I'm not sure—"

"Oh, please, Jess!" she pleaded, dropping her hands to his shoulders. "Won't you at least talk to her, to Cely Johnson, about me—once I'm strong enough to be of some use to her?"

"I suppose we could . . . think about it," he said reluctantly. At her quick smile, he added firmly, "But not for some weeks yet. You'll have to be patient."

"Oh, I will, Jess! I promise I will."

He drew her face to his and kissed her with great tenderness.

"I wonder," he finally murmured against a soft wave of her hair, "if I'll ever be able to deny you anything?"

She hugged him in reply, feeling the first glimmer of anticipation she'd known since the day their child had been lost to them. "Just don't deny me this," she said softly, more to herself than to him.

CHAPTER SIX

The first week of November brought a series of new experiences to Kerry, not all of them pleasant.

On Wednesday evening of that week she attended her first meeting of the Ladies Benevolence Society. Mrs. Northcote, as aloof and dignified as Kerry remembered, favored her with no more than a cursory glance and, later, a somewhat restrained introduction to the other women of the group. The round, nervous Mrs. Pence made an attempt to be cordial, but only when her domineering friend wasn't watching.

Many of the women made Kerry feel decidedly uncomfortable, even unwelcome. She couldn't shake the feeling that she had already been measured and found sadly lacking. Only the warm-hearted Adeline Corbett and a few of her friends gave Kerry a genuinely enthusiastic welcome.

Even before the evening was under way, Kerry fervently began to wish for its end. She longed for the comfort of Jess's strong arms, and she felt a distinct need for the benefit of his wisdom and experience to help her deal with this unexpected rejection. But when she returned home later that night, she decided to say nothing. He looked tired and seemed unusually preoccupied; obviously, the man already had more than enough on his mind without her adding an extra measure of worry.

Two days later, Mackenzie drove her to the Negro children's school on the far edge of town for her first meeting with Cely Johnson, the teacher. Her hopes were high; dozens of ideas about how she might help with the children had been scurrying through her mind for days. At first, however, it appeared as though this experience would be no more successful than her evening with the Ladies Society.

Although Jess had arranged for Kerry to meet with Cely Johnson, when the day arrived, he was unable to accompany her. Instead he had been called to the bedside of a mortally ill wife and mother.

By the time Kerry arrived at the small, white frame schoolhouse, which had a forlorn and abandoned appearance in its setting on the isolated riverbank, she was feeling very young and extremely unsure of herself. In an attempt to disguise her uncertainty, she gave Mackenzie a bright smile as he helped her from the carriage. She fluffed her skirts and patted her hair in a reassuring gesture, then asked him to come back for her later.

A mob of boisterous black children played in front of the schoolhouse. Kerry started to slowly thread her way through them. The noise broke and subsided into total silence as she followed the dirt pathway through their midst to the entrance of the building. Meeting their curious stares with a hesitant smile that was returned by only one or two of the very smallest children, she ascended the sagging wooden steps.

When she reached the weatherbeaten porch, she came to an abrupt halt. Framed in the doorway stood one of the most strikingly beautiful women Kerry had even seen. The young black woman blocking her entrance was at least a head taller than Kerry and as slender and graceful in appearance as a gazelle. Her face loked to have been struck in bronze, and her dark, severely short hairstyle emphasized her flawless features. A ruthless intelligence, as well as a definite glint of hostility, stared out at Kerry from large almond-shaped eyes.

Kerry immediately sensed the black woman's antagonism. Even

so, the teacher apparently felt it necessary to express her opinion. Within seconds, Kerry was uncomfortably aware of the fact that, to Cely Johnson, she was just one more white do-gooder who couldn't possibly be of any conceivable value to her or the children.

The teacher was brutally frank. "This isn't your typical little church school, Mrs. Dalton," she said brusquely after they introduced themselves to each other. "I'm not just in the business of teaching these children how to read and do sums." Her voice was hard. "I spend more time putting ointment on dirty, cut feet that don't have any shoes or digging up food for hungry mouths who haven't eaten for two days than I do teaching. I also delouse heads, patch worn-out pants, and occasionally handwash soiled underwear."

She stopped for a moment, twisting her wide, perfectly molded mouth into a grim line. "I have my hands full just trying to keep these children healthy enough to be here. And when winter comes, it will be harder than ever."

After a tired sigh, her voice softened a little as she continued. "Look, Mrs. Dalton, I know about your loss, and I'm really sorry for you and the preacher. He's a good man, and I'm sure you're a fine lady. But you're not going to find your standard, cute little pickaninnies here. These children are often dirty, almost always hungry, and justfiably angry. At their best, they'll probably offend your delicate sensitivities. At their worst, if you should happen to end up caring about them, they'll keep you awake nights with worry and an aching heart. Do yourself and me a favor: go back to the parsonage and help pack goodwill baskets."

Kerry stood unmoving. Feeling her temper spark and flare, she was unwilling to look away from the tall woman's commanding, level gaze. At the same time, she was reluctant to accept any further humiliation. A moment of silence hovered between them before she trusted herself to speak.

Burying her hands inside her cloak so her clenched fists couldn't be seen and lifting her chin, she replied with tightly controlled anger, "My husband told me you're a wonderful teacher, Miss Johnson. He neglected to warn me that you're also very rude."

She saw the black woman bristle but gave her no quarter.

"Obviously, my reason for wanting to work with you was severely flawed. I was under the impression, you see, that your first concern was the children, not your own insufferable independence. Would you tell me then, Miss Johnson—" Kerry's tone sharpened even as her brogue thickened. "Have I failed to meet your sterling standards because I'm Irish or because I'm white?"

Her question hung between them, suspended on a thin wire of tension. Hurt and disappointed, Kerry refused to retreat from the hard, studying glare of Cely Johnson. She fervently wished she hadn't been so quick to dismiss Mackenzie.

She knew she should say nothing more. She was angry, terribly angry—and hadn't Jess reminded her more than once that her temper was often her worst enemy. For days she had thought of nothing but this new venture; she had prayed about it, planned for it, gone over it dozens of times in her mind. Now, to have it end before it even got started was more than she was willing to accept.

Kerry was almost startled to hear herself speaking again, her voice dark and husky with emotion. "You think I'm a stranger to poverty, do you?" She uttered a small, brittle laugh. "Let me tell you, Miss, that I could most likely teach you more about poverty and dirty, starving little children than you'd ever be wanting to know."

The teacher's delicately arched eyebrows lifted with surprise, and her expression gradually softened as Kerry continued her tirade. "Can I more easily impress you, Miss Johnson, if I tell you how I found our neighbors and closest friends dead, along with their two children? Destroyed by fever and half-eaten by their own dogs, they were. Or perhaps I could better curry your favor by telling you how, as a child, I used my da's gun to shoot rats off the corpses of my childhood playmate and her Mum until we could get them decently buried." Kerry knew she must stop. Too many horrors lay just below the surface of her memories—some of which she could never bear to face again.

Suddenly, she felt extremely tired. She no longer cared about her pride, her dignity, or what Cely Johnson thought of her. She no longer cared about much of anything except getting out of there and going home. Without another word, she turned her back on the teacher and started down the steps.

A firm grasp on her shoulder caused her to stop. "Mrs. Dalton—"

Kerry turned and waited, her gaze steady and expressionless as the young black woman silently searched her eyes. Finally, with a slight twitch at one corner of her mouth, Cely drawled, "Why didn't you just tell me you were Irish to begin with?" She then smiled a full, dazzling smile as she pressed Kerry's shoulder gently and turned her around toward the schoolhouse door.

"I sure hope you know some good stories—the Irish are supposed to be great with stories, aren't they? The children say I'm a terrible storyteller."

Cely stopped long enough to pick up a small bell from the windowsill; she shook it vigorously. "You'd best brace yourself, Mrs. Dalton. Recess is over!"

Kerry did everthing wrong that first day. Anxious to impress Cely, she tried too hard and accomplished very little. But she quickly learned, with relief, that the teacher seemed to possess unlimited patience. Obviously, she intended to give Kerry all the time and guidance she might need. And by the end of the day, Kerry was convinced that poor Cely would undoubtedly find it necessary to draw on every precious scrap of that golden patience.

CHAPTER SEVEN

Following the Sunday morning service, Kerry stood beside Jess in the narthex of the church saying good-bye to the departing worshipers. In spite of the heartening affirmation she'd received from Cely Johnson at the end of her first day at the school, this morning had brought a renewed plague of old, familiar doubts and feelings of insecurity.

She was grateful for the encouraging words and friendly smiles offered by a number of church members as they left the building. Perhaps Jess was right in maintaining that most of the people had accepted her. Indeed, many had been extremely kind to both of them since their arrival.

But Kerry was certain there were many who openly resented her. Jess continued to insist that the hostility of these few had nothing to do with her personally, that the real problem lay in their opposition to his abolitionist ties and the emotionalism with which he conducted his ministry.

Kerry wasn't so sure. Most of the outright antagonism she sensed came from a number of ladies who made up the elite inner circle of Washington's society. This particular group, headed by Lydia Northcote, made no effort to disguise their disapproval of the pastor's wife.

Adeline Corbett, their kindhearted, sympathetic neighbor, approached and greeted both Kerry and Jess with genuine warmth. Laughing at the attractive older woman's comment about Molly and the mischievous new kitten, Kerry flinched with surprise when she felt Jess's firm hand grip her shoulder. She turned quickly with a questioning look, only to encounter the impassive gaze of Senator Preston Forbrush.

The diminutive, silver-haired senator was an enigma to Kerry. Although he had called on the Daltons during the latter days of Kerry's recovery and had appeared genuinely concerned for her, he was, nevertheless, a known opponent of the abolition movement—and of Jess. Kerry had found him stiffly polite, almost courtly in his manner the day he visited. Afterward, she suggested to Jess that perhaps they had misjudged the southern senator.

Jess, however, had surprised her with his statement that Forbrush was one of the most powerful and feared men in Washington. "That fine, courtly gentleman," he had stated in a tone lightly edged with distaste, "is said to have the power of life and death over most of the political careers in the country. From what I've heard, even a disagreement with him can be disastrous. He has the unsavory reputation of never forgetting a wrong and never letting go of a grudge."

A few days after the senator's visit, Jess came home one evening and glumly reported on a remark that Forbrush had supposedly made to several members of the church financial comittee about Jess being nothing more than a "young hothead who uses his pulpit as a soapbox."

Kerry had distrusted the politician ever since, and now felt acutely uncomfortable in his presence. It took only a moment, however, for her to realize that the reason for Jess's steadying grasp on her shoulder—and the present focus of his attention—wasn't Senator Forbrush, but rather the tall young man standing beside him. Slender and handsomely attired in a perfectly tailored dark suit, the man turned to meet Kerry's astonished stare with a look of amused contempt. He flicked his cold hazel eyes over her with disdain.

"How good to see you again . . . Mrs. Dalton . . . ma'am." His easy drawl was thick with undisguised sarcasm.

Lowell Martin. Kerry felt herself flush, and for a moment she was sure she was going to be ill. Her throat constricted, her hands began to tremble uncontrollably, and a think line of clammy perspiration dotted her upper lip. She was aware that Jess had draped a protective arm around her, and she reached up to cover his hand with her own, seeking even more support.

The man standing in front of her and measuring her reaction with interested scorn had been an upperclassman at West Point when Kerry arrived there as the chaplain's ward. Under the guise of escorting Kerry home one fall afternoon, he proceeded to verbally humiliate her. When his advances rapidly grew more brutal, only the intervention of a young plebe, Tom Jackson, saved Kerry from a physical assault.

Jess saw to Martin's dismissal from the Academy that very afternoon, and Kerry assumed she would never see the man again. Unbelievably, he now stood before her, looking completely at ease as he studied her with a disturbing, impudent glint in his eyes.

She was dimly aware that Jess had mumbled a grudging "Martin," and knew instantly that he had been shaken as badly as she by the unexpected meeting. Martin, however, made no effort to end the encounter, but simply smiled at both of them, allowing his insolent gaze to linger overly long on Kerry.

"What a pleasant surprise," he said smoothly, still raking Kerry with his bold, insinuating stare, "to find the two of you married. Certainly yours was a storybook romance, wasn't it? The chaplain and his ward—ah, and now the happy ending."

The look he turned on Jess was dark with a malignant undercurrent. "Naturally, Mr. Dalton, I'm delighted to see you again," he said in that same sarcastic tone. "I always held you in such . . . high regard at the Academy." He glanced slyly at Senator Forbrush. "I'm so glad the senator invited me to attend services with him this morning," he continued. "I have the privilege, you see, of being Senator Forbrush's new aide. So . . . we'll be seeing much of each other in the future, Mr. Dalton." He nodded to Kerry. "Mrs. Dalton. Certainly, I'll look forward to seeing you again."

With disbelief, Kerry watched Martin hold the dark-paneled door open for the senator; then he followed Forbrush outside.

Jess bent his head to study Kerry with concern. "Are you all right, dear?" he asked softly, giving her hand a gentle squeeze before glancing quickly at Charles Payne, his secretary, who was next in the line of departing parishioners.

Unable to speak, Kerry nodded and continued to grasp his arm in a desperate vise.

"I think Molly's out on the portico," Jess said. "Shall I take you to her so you can get some air?"

"Yes—I mean, you shouldn't leave. There are still people in the line . . . I can go alone."

"Are you sure you're all right, love?" He studied her face with an anxious frown.

Kerry nodded. She wasn't all right, of course. An overpowering surge of nausea threatened to bring her to her knees. She had to get out of here, but she mustn't make a scene . . . must not embarrass Jess. Dropping her hand from his arm, she darted a weak smile at Charles. Then, as the dark-haired young man moved to shake hands with Jess, Kerry quickly turned and made her way on trembling legs to get her cloak and go outside.

On the portico, she stood alone for a moment, glancing around uneasily at the few small groups huddled together making conversation as they prepared to leave the church. Finally, she spied Molly across the crowd and started toward her.

Too late, she realized that in order to reach the housekeeper she would have to pass between several small groups of chatting women, one of which included Lydia Northcote, Marian Pence, and two other fashionably gowned ladies from the "inner circle."

They seemed completely unaware of her presence, but Kerry couldn't help but overhear their conversation as she walked by. Their words went directly to her heart with a knifing stab of pain.

"So common, isn't she? But what else could we expect? Another Irish immigrant, you know."

Kerry recognized Mrs. Northcote's distinct, imperious voice.

66

Still smarting from the sick horror of the scene with Lowell Martin, she felt a sudden, almost vicious urge to strike out at the self-assured, smug face of the society matron. Instead, she continued to make her way between the groups, determined not to hear another word.

But when Mrs. Pence murmured something about the Dalton lineage reportedly being "extremely noble," Kerry again slowed her pace.

"Well, there won't be a continuance of that . . . noble lineage, will there?" Lydia Northcote's haughty remark sounded much like a sneer. "I have been told," she said importantly, through a delicate grimace of distaste, "that she is now . . . barren."

There were a few deep breaths of surprise, then Marian Pence asked timidly, "Wherever did you hear that, Lydia?"

Lydia Northcote was obviously unaccustomed to having her pronouncements questioned. She rebuked her companion with a withering glare, cleared her throat lightly, and continued. "I have my sources, Marian, as I'm sure you're aware. And I was told that the woman went running through the street like a savage—ran until she dropped, they say. Not only did she lose the child—" She lowered her voice meaningfully. "But I was told that she can have no others."

Kerry's gasp of stricken astonishment caused the cluster of women to turn in unison and gape at her.

Marian Pence colored fiercely and uttered a weak, "Lydia—"

Mrs. Northcote silently studied the dismayed Kerry without a hint of contrition softening her gaze. If she felt any remorse at all, she effectively concealed it by simply lifting one patrician brow before turning away with deliberate indifference.

Kerry desperately wanted to run but refused to let them see the devastating result of their cruelty. She knew she was dangerously close to total collapse, but she would contain herself at all costs. It would be abject humiliation for poor Jess if she were to make a spectacle of herself right here in front of the church building.

She stood, unmoving, staring at the cluster of women until the entire group silently turned away from her and walked off the portico. Drawing a deep, steadying breath, Kerry resolutely fixed her attention on Molly, who was talking with Adeline Corbett, both of them obviously unaware of the scene that had just taken place.

When Kerry finally reached Molly's side, she grasped the housekeeper's stout forearm and said tightly, "Please, Molly, could we go to the carriage? I'm feeling a bit wobbly, I'm afraid."

Molly looked from Kerry to Mrs. Corbett with concern but wasted no time in tucking Kerry's arm through hers and firmly guiding her to the carriage where Mackenzie stood waiting.

Jess appeared moments later, having changed out of his clerical robe and into a black greatcoat. Quickly getting in beside Kerry, he put an arm around her and pulled her close to him. "Mrs. Corbett said you're not feeling well. Is it because of Martin, dear?" he asked with concern. "Did he upset you that much?"

Leaning against him, Kerry hesitated. She wanted to tell him everything, but should she add even more to the burden he was already carrying? What good would come of it? What exactly could Jess do? Nothing, she realized with grim resignation. There was absolutely nothing Jess—or anyone else—could do. While it was true that he had a way of making things better once he put a hand to them, he was powerless to change what his wife was or where she had come from.

Her decision made, Kerry nodded a silent agreement to his question about Martin; she kept her silence about everything else.

That night, Jess walked into their bedroom and found Kerry sitting at her dressing table braiding her hair with fierce, determined movements. He stood just inside the door a moment, watching her, then walked over and placed his hands on her shoulders.

He silently studied her reflection in the oval mirror, then pulled up a chair behind her and sat down. His warm, fond gaze met hers in the mirror. "Let me do that, love. You're going to yank all your curls out," he teased.

Kerry gave the job over to him with a restless sigh.

"Do you know," he asked softly, smiling at her reflection, "that the only time you ever braid your hair is when you're worried or upset?"

She looked surprised, then relaxed a little. "Da used to say that you must occupy anxious hands or they'll stir a pot of trouble."

He chuckled. "Dear one, it will take more than braids to keep those little hands of yours from doing a bit of stirring, I believe. Anyway," he declared abruptly, "you know I don't like your hair braided."

He gently separated the thickly coiled braid, touching his lips as he did so to one stubborn copper curl intent upon flopping over her ear. Picking up a hairbrush from the dressing table, he began to slowly brush her hair with sure, even strokes.

With dismay, he saw her chin tremble and her green eyes mist with unshed tears. "Kerry, sweetheart, what's wrong? Are you still worried about Martin? I won't let him near you again, I promise you that."

She shook her head in protest, knowing she had no answer for him; the day had simply been too much. His dependable, loving gentleness had broken through the wall she'd erected earlier and threatened to crumble her well-intentioned defenses.

"I'm sorry, Jess . . . I don't know what's wrong with me tonight. I must be tired."

He returned the brush to the dressing table. Dropping both hands to her shoulders, he turned her around to face him. "Here, love," he prompted softly, gathering her closer and tucking her head against the hollow of his shoulder. "Are you sure there's nothing wrong?"

Again she shook her head, unwilling to meet his searching gaze. "Why is it, I wonder," she said dully, her voice muffled in the cool silk of his dressing gown, "that the more I want to please you, the more burden I seem to be to you?"

"Hush, now, love. That's simply not true," he reassured her in a soft but firm voice. Carefully, he scooped her up into his arms and carried her over to the rocking chair by the hearth where flames were gently lapping at the large, fragrant logs in the fireplace. He sat down and settled her comfortably on his lap. "My foolish, darling girl," he murmured against her temple as he began to rock slowly back and forth in the sturdy chair. "Don't you know by now that you are always infinitely pleasing to me? Why, all you have to do is draw a breath to make me happy."

"Oh, Jess, you always say the very thing to make me feel better, but more and more I see the ways I'm failing you, and it hurts me, knowing how much you deserve and how little I can give you."

Frowning with protest, Jess drew his face away from her. "Don't ever say that, dear love of my heart." He strengthened his protective embrace almost fiercely, holding Kerry so tightly that she almost lost her breath against his solid chest.

"You have never, ever failed me! Not once! And you never will. You could only fail me if you were to stop loving me."

"That could never be, my treasure," Kerry whispered against him.

She tipped her head to look up at him, then lifted her hands and placed them tenderly on either side of his face. Her words were a smothered promise as she gazed directly into his eyes. "I could no more stop loving you than I could stop the breath leaving my body, cuisle mo chroid."*

She lost herself in the sweetness of his love-softened expression, the exquisite tenderness of his touch, the fervent reassurance of his kiss. When he raised his lips from hers, he searched her eyes, his gaze brimming with adoration and yearning.

"Kerry . . . are you well enough . . . can we love?" he murmured hoarsely.

In answer, she pulled his head down closer to her face and smiled into his love-filled eyes. She nodded almost shyly.

He saw her expression abruptly sober with anxious regret. "Is it going to make a difference, Jess . . that I can no longer give you a child?"

His eyes misted. She was like a small, wounded animal uncertain of her worth. He knew this question had been burning in her heart for weeks. There was such a heaviness in his chest he nearly cried out with the pain of it.

Somehow, he stilled his own aching heart and let all the intensity of his love shine out to her. He attempted to draw her troubled spirit into himself by the very force of his gaze. Then, lifting her in his arms, he rose carefully from the chair, his eyes never leaving her face. "Nothing," he promised in a husky whisper, "will ever make a difference in our love."

He cradled her closely against him and brushed one soft kiss of reassurance across her forehead before carrying her across the room.

CHAPTER EIGHT

Kerry could hear the call of winter in the late November wind howling through the old oaks outside their bedroom window. The angry, moaning wail made her feel sad and alone even though Jess was sleeping soundly beside her. In a week, they would celebrate Thanksgiving. She admitted to herself that her increasing heaviness of heart was due, at least in part, to the approaching holidays.

For Jess's sake, she made every effort to be cheerful; most of the time, she succeeded. It was impossible, however, for her to forget that only a few months ago they had discussed this year's holiday season with great anticipation, certain it would be the most joyous ever for both of them.

Their baby was to have been born in December. They had hoped for a Christmas baby who might share the Savior's birthday. Now she was afraid the holidays would only bring pain in remembering all they had lost.

With a restless sigh, Kerry turned her face toward the window and stared woodenly at the faint trickle of moonlight filtering in through the drapes. She knew it was wrong to feel this way; her gloomy attitude most likely grieved the Lord. But, try as she would, she could not shake the oppressive feeling that a storm was gathering on the horizon of their future, a storm that would somehow shake the very foundation of their lives. Sometimes, she felt as if the death of their child had been only the beginning, a dreadful, heart-wounding prelude to an impending disaster.

With an involuntary shudder, she turned to study Jess's face, shadowed and barely visible in the faint glow of moonlight hovering about their bed. As always, his arms were wrapped around her in a snug, protective embrace. Lifting her hand to gently brush a springy wave of hair away from his forehead, Kerry smiled sadly as she pressed a tender kiss to his bearded cheek and then rested her head in the hollow of his shoulder.

Oh, Jess . . . asthore* . . . what does the future hold for us? What is this frightening city going to mean to our lives together, to our marriage?

Of late it seemed to Kerry that she was terribly ungrateful, no more than a spoiled child. Didn't she have more, far more than most women ever dream of?

The powerful but gentle giant sleeping beside her was a true man of God, an unshakable tower of a man. Some of the most influential newspapermen and publishers in the North had referred to Jess in such glowing terms as "brilliant," "a man on fire," "a man who wields a pen of power and a pulpit of change." Hadn't Mr. Henry Ward Beecher himself gone so far as to call Jess a nineteenth-century prophet?

And yet he loved her—had loved her, so he said, since she was no more than a slip of a girl in a gingham dress and a tattered shawl. He had given her a place in his life, in his home, and in his heart. He had taken her in, cared for her, protected her, educated her—and finally married her.

Oh, and didn't she love him, too? I love him more than everything, Lord, you know that. Sometimes my heart feels about to burst with love for him, it does. Why, then, am I hurting so? Why can't I simply be satisfied with things as they are? Why can't I let go of the grief about the babe? And why does it squeeze my heart so that there are those who seem to count me as worthless, who look upon me as no more than "Irish riffraff?" Why should it

72

matter what anyone else thinks, so long as my Jess loves me?

He would be furious and terribly hurt if he were to know the extent of the rejection and insulting treatment she had suffered from Lydia Northcote and the others. And that was exactly why she had chosen to keep silent. Surely she could handle this alone, without running to him as she was used to doing with each and every petty problem.

Lately he'd been besieged with a mountain of cares and concerns, an increasing load of responsibilities and burdens; he seemed engulfed by the problems of others. In addition to the voluminous duties of his pastorate, a growing number of politicians now came seeking his counsel. And he had his writing, too. Jess was never without a book in progress, and Kerry's head still reeled at the way his prolific pen could pour out dozens of articles for newspapers while fashioning a sermon that would leave one shaken for days.

No, she had been right to remain silent about her own problems. After all, she was no stranger to disapproval and suspicion. Hadn't she encountered it often enough in the hostile streets of Buffalo where she and her da had lived when they first came to America?

Even at West Point, she had experienced the pain of rejection. The contemptuous assault of Lowell Martin served as a reminder that there would always be those who viewed her, and "her kind," as less than acceptable.

For Jess's sake, she would handle this alone. It was all so insignificant, really, considering the far more important matters he encountered almost daily. This much, at least, she could spare him.

Kerry turned restlessly in his arms, trying not to wake him. Lately, her sleep had been fitful at best. Often, her thoughts and questioning emotions kept her awake for hours after they retired. Now that the wind had quieted, she felt a welcome blanket of drowsiness settle over her. Burrowing more closely against Jess's large, solid warmth, she finally slept.

In the small, dark cottage behind the parsonage, Mackenzie reluctantly opened his eyes and lay still for a few moments as he tried to figure out what had awakened him. Finally, he sat up, yawned, and slowly swung his feet over the side of the bed. Grumbling irritably, he scratched his head and waited, listening.

There it was; he had heard something. Sure, and weren't the mares snorting and carrying on in the carriage house?

With a tired grunt, he hauled himself into a pair of trousers over his union suit, hiked up his suspenders, and put on his shoes. He went to the small window and peered out across the few feet separating him from the carriage house. A thin stream of moonlight zigzagged across the lawn, but he saw nothing.

Still, the horses were afret about something; he'd best look in on them. The youngest was a feisty one, easily put off her feed, but he'd see to her, just to be sure. The little missus favored her something fierce.

Almost as an afterthought, he went back to the bed and pulled a shillelagh from beneath it. Shrugging into his woolen work coat and hobbling stiffly out the back door of the bungalow, he crossed to the rear of the carriage house. He stopped once thinking he heard something at the front of the yard. Seeing nothing, he shuffled on toward the carriage house and entered through the back door.

Mib, the older gray, was reasonably placid, paying him little attention. The small black mare, however, was obviously nervous, her eyes wild and her ears pricked stiffly forward as the breath from her nostrils steamed the cold air in the stall.

"And what might be biting at you, you young she-devil?" he growled affectionately while stroking and soothing her with his large hand and droning voice.

In moments, he had gentled her enough that she consented to nuzzle a bit of sugar from the small supply he always kept in his pockets. "Well now, and are we ready to take another snooze? It's heavy these old peepers of mine are. You've already cost me a good—"

He stopped and whirled around at the sound of a nearby shout—a shout soon followed by another. He heard a thud and a sudden crackling. The mare went crazy, and even the sluggish gray began to whinny and toss her head in agitation.

Mackenzie glanced at the shillelagh in his hand then moved as

74

fast as his arthritic legs would take him to the front entrance of the carriage house. From there, he could see his cottage no more than a few feet away.

The sight that greeted him chilled his blood and made his once-drowsy eyes widen with stunned alarm. He had the presence of mind to flatten himself against the wall by the doorway where he could look out without being seen.

His small bungalow was in flames. The blaze was already high enough to shed a bright halo of light about the cottage and above the rooftop. Framed in the glow of the fire, four hooded, dark-cloaked men sat on horseback and silently watched the cottage burn. In the shadowy light from the flames, Mackenzie could see that all four were armed with rifles.

He clutched the shillelagh tighter and glanced anxiously around the carriage house. In a sick rage, he realized he was helpless. The oaken cudgel in his hand would be useless against the armed men.

Smoke began to burn his eyes and lungs as he stood unmoving, watching the little house he'd become extremely fond of over the years burn to the ground.

Lord, Lord, don't let the family wake, he prayed silently. Keep them safe inside, for now at least!

He expelled a deep breath of relief when he saw the four men abruptly turn their horses, at the instruction of the rider in the middle, and go thundering off into the night. He then ran as fast as he could toward the main house, shouting as he raced across the yard. "Fire! There's a fire!"

He stopped at the back porch steps and bent to pick up a rock. Hoisting a metal bucket from beside the porch, he started banging wildly and yelling at the top of his lungs.

Molly was the first out the back door, screaming as she charged off the porch, her unsecured braids tossing to and fro, her brown bathrobe flapping as she ran. She stopped a few feet away from the porch and stood paralyzed, staring in shocked disbelief at the blazing cottage.

Go sabhala Dia sinn!* She launched into her native Gaelic for a swift prayer, then began to cry out Mackenzie's name. Panicking, she started to run, and turned in mid-stride, looking wildly upward to the second floor of the house. "Jess! Come quickly! Mackenzie's place is on fire!"

Jess, however, was already on his way. He shot through the door, dressed only in his pants and boots, throwing on a coat as he ran. Kerry was right behind him, struggling with the belt on her dressing gown as she ran outdoors.

"Stop your screaming, old woman!" Mackenzie roared at the housekeeper, grabbing her arm from behind which caused Molly to scream even louder. She whirled around to face Mackenzie, gave one final yelp, then hushed, looking from the caretaker to the burning cottage.

"You—you're not inside, then!" she stammered blankly.

"Sure, and I'm not!" Mackenzie growled acidly. "Get a bucket now! We must take the buckets to the pond!"

Kerry ran up to the caretaker and grasped his arm as if to reassure herself that he wasn't inside the burning building. "Mackenzie! Oh, Mackenzie—you're all right, then?"

"I'm perfectly fine, missus," he said gruffly, flustered and pleased by her concern. He turned from her and started for the pond with a bucket.

"Kerry, go back inside!" Jess ordered, grabbing a bucket for himself. "You'll catch cold out here!"

"No! You'll be needing me to help, too!" she shouted back at him.

For over two hours they worked furiously bailing water from the pond behind the cottage and flinging it onto the blaze. The smell of smoke and all the noise attracted several neighbors who came to help. A small volunteer fire company also showed up, too late to be of any real assistance.

The wind settled, and they finally succeeded in extinguishing the blaze, but the cottage was destroyed. Only a charred shell of one wall remained standing.

Much later, after they'd answered numerous questions from the firemen and the police, the four of them sat in the kitchen drinking coffee and talking in hushed, disturbed tones. Their faces were grimy, their hair and clothing saturated with the smell of smoke. But they were simply too tired to care.

Jess had no answer when both Kerry and Molly asked about

the reason for the fire. A number of possibilities occurred to him, all of them troubling.

It was Mackenzie who finally made a terse reply. "I'm thinking we'd best take it as a warning," he said, his words dropping heavily into the silence around the large pine table.

"A warning?" Kerry asked, glancing uncertainly at Jess.

"Aye, and perhaps even more," Mackenzie replied, raising his head to look directly into Kerry's eyes. "I'm a known Irisher, missus—same as you." Without looking at her, he nodded toward Molly and added grudgingly, "Her, too."

Ignoring the housekeeper's glare, he continued. "The cottage is but a few feet from the house where you and the pastor were sleeping, don't you see?"

Kerry and Molly stared in bewilderment at Mackenzie. Jess, uncomfortable with his own suspicions, kept his eyes focused on the coffee cup in front of him.

"They likely thought I was inside," Mackenzie went on, his tone heavy with fatigue. "And that didn't bother them at all, now, did it?" He looked pointedly at Jess, who finally raised his head and met the caretaker's worried gaze.

"I'm thinking this bunch, whoever they may be, aren't a bit squeamish about harming an Irisher—especially one associated with the pastor."

Jess was unwilling—or afraid—to agree with Mackenzie, as if merely giving voice to his fears would make them more a reality. Still, he asked the question that had clawed at his mind since the terror of this night began: "You think this was meant as a threat against Kerry?" he asked quietly while he reached to cover her hand with his.

Mackenzie cocked his head and pursed his wide mouth. "I'd be inclined to think, Pastor," he said slowly, "that it was a threat against the two of you. Aye, that's what it looks like to me."

Kerry and Molly traded uneasy glances but said nothing. The four remained in unbroken silence for a long time. If any one of them had an opinion about Mackenzie's comment, no one voiced it. Occasionally, Jess looked over at Kerry sitting beside him, and once Molly narrowed her eyes and measured the caretaker with an appraising stare. But no one spoke until Jess asked Molly to prepare one of the bedrooms in the back of the house for Mackenzie.

"You can move into the house for now, Mack," he offered, "until we get the cottage rebuilt."

When the older man protested saying he could get a room in a boardinghouse, Jess firmly silenced him.

"I'd feel better, Mack, with another man in the house, especially since I'm gone so much. I'd really like for you to stay close."

Mackenzie searched Jess's eyes for a moment, then nodded his assent. Lifting his chin, he turned a defiant stare on Molly, as if he expected her to challenge Jess's suggestion.

Molly, however, simply curled her lip in an expression of resigned disgust, rolled her eyes toward heaven—and remained unexpectedly silent.

CHAPTER NINE

The Sunday before Thanksgiving, Kerry sat on the edge of her pew and listened to Jess deliver a sermon which would, she suspected uneasily, ruffle a few feathers. But only those who deserve to have them ruffled a bit, she reminded herself.

He creatively threaded his message around the arrival of the pilgrims in America, the aid given them by the Indians, and the relationships—the friendships—that developed between many of the early settlers and the "savages" they had been taught to fear. He told how the descendants of those same pilgrims later plundered the lands of the very ones who had helped their ancestors, detailing a number of ways that "Americans abused Americans."

"And we're still doing it," he said quietly, with a sad, knowing smile. "What a shock it must be," he continued gravely, "to those who, for years, have thought of themselves as being decent, ordinary people—acceptable to God and presumably to the rest of the human race—to discover that they're not what they thought they were because the color of their skin is different or because there's a burr or a brogue in their speech or because their religion isn't what others think it should be. Imagine their astonishment when they realize that God must not consider them a part of his creation after all, even though they're strikingly similar to the rest of us who are walking around claiming to belong to Him."

Kerry stared up at him, wide-eyed and a little surprised—as always—while her gentle-natured husband took on the mantle of power and eloquence he wore so easily once he faced a congregation. They had been married for nearly three years, and she had watched him and listened to him expound from his pulpit almost every Sunday during that time, yet she never failed to feel a sense of awe and wonder at the towering, black-robed figure he presented as he spoke to the people of his pastorate. Sometimes quiet-voiced, sometimes fiery; occasionally sorrowful, always sincere; frequently challenging, never condemning, Jess was a man who had dedicated himself to making a difference for God.

And he did make a difference, Kerry thought to herself with pride, allowing her mind to drift back to West Point. Most of the cadets at the Academy had thought of Jess as a rock, a stronghold. Rare was the man who graduated from West Point during the years Jess served as chaplain who didn't at least once, according to Molly, rely on his advice or assistance in some way.

And he was making a difference in Washington, too, Kerry believed, though it hadn't been easy for him. The Polk administration was known to be far more concerned about expansion and national power than the issue of human rights. Indeed, President Polk himself had been accused by some of the leading reformers in the country of being indifferent to the issue of slavery, the hardships of the factory workers, and the poverty of thousands of immigrants. Others regarded the stern-faced president as no more than a tool of the slave owners. Even Jess, usually quick to give every man the benefit of the doubt, admitted that the present chief executive seemed less than concerned about the country's social problems.

The current political regime's focus on the "manifest destiny" of the nation seemed to leave little time or energy to consider the plight of the laborers who were helping settle and build the country into the world power envisioned by the politicians. Consequently, Jess's crusade for a higher quality of life for the impoverished and enslaved was often ignored or viewed with disdain and anger by the majority of those with political influence.

But there were those who listened, and some were beginning to think for themselves. Opinions were changing, hearts were softening, and steps were being taken—although they were slow and often uncertain—to put into motion those laws that would eventually guarantee a better life for all Americans.

Kerry knew Jess was attempting to gain an audience with the Senate, hoping to inspire and encourage those who had the necessary influence and power to use it for the suffering, oppressed masses. But she also knew he had begun to despair of ever having his request granted. The few senators who agreed with Jess's views had strong opponents in most of the southern senators. Northcote, Forbrush, Calhoun, and others made no secret of the fact that they considered Jess to be hopelessly naive, even foolish.

Jess was a man ordinarily pleased with even the smallest signs of progress in his endeavors. Kerry often marveled at his seemingly bottomless reservoir of patience. Lately, however, she worried more than a little about his frequent fatigued appearance and occasional periods of brooding. He was given to long silences—which she'd grown used to. But this was different.

Ever since Mackenzie's cottage had burned down, Jess remained uncommonly quiet and heavy-spirited. When she questioned him, he would simply shrug off his melancholy and quickly make a cheerful effort to reassure her. She wasn't convinced, however. He was obviously troubled but apparently determined not to worry her.

Realizing that her thoughts had wandered far from the sermon, Kerry colored guiltily when a sudden, unusual silence jolted her back to the present. She turned her attention to the pulpit, only to see Jess staring out into the congregation with a peculiar frown of dismay.

A quiet stirring had begun throughout the sanctuary; heads turned and voices whispered as a number of people craned their necks to see what was happening. Jess's last few words died abruptly on his lips, and Kerry saw a flush shadow his face.

Uneasily, she turned her gaze in the direction of his disconcerted stare, catching her breath sharply when she saw that Senator

Forbrush, the Northcotes, and Senator Calhoun and his wife had risen from their pews and were making their way up the center aisle, clearly intent on leaving the worship service.

John Calhoun, the tall, gray-haired senator from South Carolina, appeared to be pale with anger, his always severe features now hardened to a wintry mask. Not one of the departing group looked to either side of the aisle as they exited.

Once they were gone, every gaze returned to Jess in obvious anticipation of how he would deal with the blatant insult that had just been dealt him. Kerry swallowed with great difficulty and clutched her gloved hands so tightly they grew numb. She stared up at Jess. Her heart ached for his embarrassment; she desperately wanted to leave her pew and go to him.

While she sat there hurting for him, she saw his face settle into its familiar expression of quiet, controlled strength. In an even, steady tone, he continued, as if nothing out of the ordinary had taken place.

"Beloved brethren, these are not my words, but those of our Lord: 'Ye are all the children of God by faith in Christ Jesus. There is neither bond nor free. Ye are all one. God is no respector of persons—have we not all one Father? Hath not one God created us? Why do we deal treacherously every man against his brother, by profaning the covenant of our fathers?'"

He leaned far across the pulpit, his face contorted with eloquent anguish. His voice was so quiet it could be heard only with effort.

"People, please hear me. God does not see race. He doesn't see the color of our skin. God does not see our nationality or our history or our legacy. God doesn't see kings or princes, prime ministers or presidents. He doesn't see rich or poor, wise or simple, great or small. God sees . . . the heart."

He paused, caught a breath, then continued in a voice hoarse with emotion. "He isn't looking for people who meet particular standards or specifications. He isn't looking for people to judge or condemn or punish. He's looking for people to love—people who will love him in return. That's all he wants. That's all he's ever wanted."

There was a silence—a tense, waiting silence, heavy with expec-

82

tation. Jess passed the back of his hand across his eyes then turned and stepped slowly down from the pulpit, exiting through the side door of the platform rather than going to the back of the sanctuary to greet the departing congregation as he usually did. After an awkward silence, the organizst moved into a faltering postlude.

Kerry hurried from her pew, taking no notice of the excited whisperings and murmurings about her. She nearly stumbled in her haste to get out the side door and make her way to Jess's office at the rear of the building.

She found him standing at the large, narrow window behind his desk, still in his robe. When he turned to her, his shoulders were slumped and there was such an anguished look of defeat engraved upon his face she could have cried for him.

She went to him at once and stood on tiptoe to rest her hands on his shoulders; she kissed him lightly on the cheek. "I'm so terribly proud of you, dearest," she said softly. "That was a wonderful message."

He attempted a weak smile and touched one hand gently to her face. "Obviously, not everyone shared your enthusiasm, love."

"Don't let that blind bunch of bigots upset you a bit, d'you hear, Jess?" She put her arms around his middle and held him tightly, their positions reversed for once as she attempted to comfort him. Tipping her head back to gaze up at him, she added, "They're only a few, after all."

Jess shook his head ruefully. "But a most significant few, I'm afraid. I'm especially bothered by John Calhoun's attitude," he continued after a heavy sigh. "He's an intelligent man and an effective senator—one of the most powerful men in the Senate, as a matter of fact. We're at extreme odds with each other in what we believe—but I can't help but respect the man."

He sighed again, then wrapped his arms more tightly around her and rested his chin on top of her head. "Sometimes it all seems so . . . futile. So much of the problem exists because of nothing more substantial than family custom or the tradition of a particular locale. I think that's one of the things I find the most discouraging: so many people believe in slavery because their parents upheld it or because of where they were raised. It would simply never occur to them to think for themselves."

"And they despise those who are different—the Irish included—for just as little reason," Kerry murmured with understanding. "But it's as you once told me, is it not, Jess?" she asked, putting her hands on his shoulders and drawing back just enough to look up at him. "A man can do no more than speak the truth. Only the good Lord can open the ears of those who need to hear it."

He smiled down at her. "Did I say that, wife?"

"Aye, that you did, my fine husband."

He stared at her for a moment, then tipped her chin upward with one finger, his expression brightening as he looked into her eyes. "Then it must be true, I suppose."

"I should think so, sir," she returned pertly.

"Ah, Kerry . . . let's go home," he said, easing back from their embrace to shrug out of his robe. "I intend to do nothing else today but go home and stuff myself on whatever Molly's cooked up for Sunday dinner. And I don't want to think about anything more weighty than the extra two or three pounds I'm sure to put on this afternoon."

Relieved, Kerry took his robe from him and hung it in the closet. "That won't be difficult to do, dearest. I happen to know what Molly's planning for dinner."

His interest quickened as he turned back to her. "Oh? Something special?"

She shrugged and rolled her eyes mysteriously. "I'll not be spoiling her surprise. But it might just be something of which you're extremely fond."

"Dumplings?" he asked hopefully. "Did she make apple dumplings?"

With a smug smile, Kerry arched her brows, tucked her arm in his, and pulled him along behind her through the office door. "The sooner we get home, the sooner you'll be knowing, now isn't that right?"

After they finished dinner and Jess had moaned and protested enough about his overeating to please Molly, who had indeed prepared his favorite dish of apple dumplings, he and Kerry went into the library.

Kerry played with Brian Boru in front of the fire while Jess caught up on the mail and newspapers he hadn't had time to read for the past several days.

"I told you there was a letter here from John O'Sullivan, didn't I?" Jess asked, scanning the first page of several sheets of stationery.

O'Sullivan was the editor of a popular expansionist magazine; he had also been credited with first coining the phrase "manifest destiny," which had quickly gained popularity not only in Washington but throughout the entire country. Jess and O'Sullivan had become acquaintances, then friends, through their mutual contacts in publishing.

"Aye, you did," Kerry answered distractedly, laughing as she watched the rambunctious kitten tumble over his own feet and scoot across the hearth in pursuit of a catnip mouse. She was pleased to see that, true to her initial prediction for him, the tabby was growing up large and solid and brave—too brave for Molly, Kerry thought with amusement. Hardly a day passed that Brian Boru and the housekeeper didn't square off at least once. Overall, Kerry would have to judge Brian the definite winner in their contests.

"He confirms what we've been told about the potato blight in Ireland," Jess said in a low voice. "It's bad; very bad."

Alert to the note of concern in his tone, Kerry got up from the floor and went to sit beside him, perching on the arm of the sofa.

"How bad?"

He shook his head as he continued to read. "Someone in his family went over recently to check on their relatives. O'Sullivan says it would appear to be even worse than the crop failure in '39." He glanced up at her. "That's the year you left Ireland."

She nodded. "It was a terrible time. Da always tried to keep a few small crops in besides the potatoes to help us along, though the neighbors thought him odd for it. Mostly, the people live on their potatoes alone, you know."

"You can read this for yourself, but I'm afraid it's all bad news, love. John seems to think it means unavoidable disaster for Ireland, though the British government is already saying the facts have been exaggerated."

"Well, and they would," Kerry said indignantly. "Old Orange Peel* would no doubt like the country to starve to death before anyone could be knowing enough to help, disliking the Irish as he does."

Jess finished the letter then passed it to Kerry, who read it in silence. Finally, she dropped it into her lap and stared down at the floor for a long moment. "It will be famine again. And, from the sound of it, worse than ever before."

Jess reached for her hand. "I thank God you're here with me, love."

She turned her gaze onto him. "As do I, Jess. But I can't help thinking of all those who will starve to death or die in a ditch of the fever because they've no one to help them."

"England will simply have to help. She has too much invested in Ireland to ignore this."

"England's way of helping," Kerry replied with a small, bitter sound of derision, "will be to order the landlords to tumble the cottages around the very heads of starving children and send those who are still able to walk on their way to the poorhouse! That's always been the way of it, and most likely it won't be changing."

He studied her face, watching her eyes spark with anger as her brogue thickened. "John says it will be months before the full consequences of the blight are felt," he remarked, lifting another envelope from the stack on the table beside the sofa.

"That's true," Kerry agreed. "First there will be plenty. The people will be anxious to get rid of their potatoes while they can still be eaten. But after a few months, there will be nothing. That's when the hunger will start. I remember Da talking at night by the fire about other times of famine."

She handed the letter to him and rose from the arm of the sofa, walking across the room to scoop up Brian Boru from his stance in front of the window, where he was appraising the drapes for possible climbing. The kitten flattened himself against Kerry's shoulder as she straightened to look out the window into the darkness of the early winter's evening.

Molly walked in just then with a fresh pot of coffee.

"Ah, Molly, how you spoil us," Jess said, leaning back against the cushion of the sofa with a broad smile.

"You can do with a bit of spoiling today, I'm thinking," the housekeeper muttered, placing the tray on the library table behind the couch.

"Kerry have you extended our invitation to Cely for Thanksgiving dinner yet?" Jess asked.

Kerry turned around, smiling at the purring kitten nestled against her shoulder. "Aye, I did." Her expression sobered as she set the kitten to the floor. "But she won't be coming."

"Why not?"

"Well, she didn't exactly say as much," Kerry replied with a small frown, "but I believe she thought it might cause trouble for us. She hemmed and hawed and finally thanked me but said she was going to fix a meal at the school for the students and their families."

Jess looked surprised. "Where will she find the means to do that? She can't possibly afford it on her own."

Kerry crossed her arms over her chest and sighed. "It will be meager at best, I should think. But I'm coming to learn that when Cely Johnson makes up her mind to do something, she'll somehow find a way to get it done."

Jess took the cup of steaming coffee Molly held out to him. "Would she let us help, do you think?"

"Help? How could we help, Jess?"

He took a sip of coffee, then set the cup on the lamp table beside him. "Well, if Molly's willing, we could help prepare some of the food, then deliver it to the school. In fact," he said thoughtfully, "we could join Cely and the others and have dinner with them, if you'd want."

"You'd do that, Jess?" Kerry's eyes lighted with pleased surprise.

"I'd enjoy it," he replied quickly. "And you'd like being with the children, wouldn't you?"

"Oh, yes, you know I would! But—"

"Molly, would you and Mack be willing to ignore the inconvenience and help out that day?"

Molly nodded firmly without hesitation. "'Twould be no problem at all for me, but I'd not be speaking for that sour old man.

87

His mood changes with the hour, it does."

Kerry met Jess's grin with one of her own. Her expression quickly sobered, however, with her next question. "Could it bring trouble for you, though, Jess?" she asked, tugging anxiously at her fingers. "I wouldn't want to be doing anything to cause more problems than we've already had."

Seeing her eyes light with an uncertain glint of hopefulness, Jess promptly reassured her. "How could anyone fault me for helping to provide a Thanksgiving meal for a group of school children, Kerry? Besides," he added dryly, "it's not likely that we'll be running into any of the more prestigious members of the—"

His last words died on his lips, interrupted by a cry of surprised alarm as the tall, spacious window directly behind Kerry suddenly shattered. Shards of glass flew inward, as a large rock sailed into the room and hit Kerry on the head with a sickening thud.

Jess lunged forward off the couch and hurled himself directly at Kerry, shouting her name. Molly, too, charged across the room. Both were too late. Kerry was down, first on her knees, then sprawled face forward on the floor.

Mackenzie came running into the library. "What happ—" He stopped dead when he saw Kerry on the floor with Jess and Molly bent over her.

Jess's face was a stricken mask when he raised his head and turned toward Mackenzie. "Mack, go for Dr. Marshall!" When he looked back at Kerry, he nearly strangled from the tight fist of fear clutching at his throat.

But Kerry raised one hand in weak protest, moaned, and started to turn over. "No . . . I'm all right . . ."

"Careful . . . careful, love . . . there's glass all around you," Jess cautioned in a shaky voice as he helped her turn over on her back.

His hand trembled as he smoothed her hair away from her forehead and studied her face. "Thank the Lord," he murmured with relief. "I was afraid you'd been cut." Carefully, he began to pick tiny slivers of glass from the skirt of her dress.

"No, I'm fine, really," Kerry assured him, her own voice unsteady. "Just . . . my knees, I think. I must have banged them when I fell."

"But your head—"

"It's only a bump." She made a weak dismissing motion with her hand. "I'm all right."

"Well, let's get you onto the sofa for now," Jess insisted, scooping her up into his arms with extreme care. "I still want to have George Marshall look at you."

"That's not necessary, Jess. I'm fine. Just let me rest a bit."

Mackenzie and Molly followed them to the sofa and continued to hover nearby. The big, awkward caretaker stared down at Kerry with dismay.

"You sure you don't need the doctor, missus? Maybe you're hurt more than you're knowing?"

Kerry managed a smile for him. "No, Mackenzie—really, I'm fine." She shuddered slightly. "Perhaps it frightened me a bit, but that's all."

"Molly, you stay here with her," Jess said. "We're going to have a look outside."

"No, Jess!" Kerry cried, thrusting herself upward to clutch his arm. "Someone might still be out there!"

"That's exactly what I intend to find out," Jess grated, gently but firmly removing her hand from his forearm. "Mack, get your club and go with me, please."

Whoever had thrown the rock was gone by the time Jess and Mackenzie reached the yard. They searched the area in front and back of the house; they even checked the carriage house. There was nothing to be found.

Mackenzie absently swung the shillelagh from his fingers and shook his head gloomily as they walked back into the house. "Do you suppose someone really meant to hurt the little missus, Pastor?" he asked, stopping in the reception hall. "Or is it just another threat, do you think?"

Jess felt extremely tired—tired and frightened and furious. He raked one hand through his hair in a gesture of frustration. "I don't know what to think anymore, Mack," he answered, dragging in a long, ragged breath, "except that perhaps I made a terrible mistake by coming here in the first place. Kerry's had nothing but misery and trouble ever since—" He stopped, unable to continue.

Mackenzie glanced at him. An uncommon warmth softened his features when he touched Jess lightly on the shoulder and mumbled reassuringly, "I'll help you take care of her, Pastor. I'll watch over her, too, just as closely as I can."

Jess searched the older man's gaze for a moment, then smiled weakly and nodded. "I know you will, Mack. And it helps me a great deal to know that."

But would it help Kerry? he silently asked himself. Was anything other than leaving Washington going to help Kerry?

CHAPTER TEN

For the first time since their nightmare began, Jess and Kerry received word from the police that they might have a witness who could be of some help, at least in a minor way.

The day after the rock was thrown through the Daltons' window, all nearby residents were questioned. One of them, an elderly man who lived on the opposite side of the Square from the parsonage, thought he "might have seen something peculiar" the night before.

He had opened his front door to call his dog and was standing in the doorway, waiting, when he thought he saw a large, dark shadow fleeing the side yard of the parsonage.

He told the investigating officer he hadn't thought much about it because he didn't see very well anymore and because "it's always so dark over there with all those big old trees." But he admitted that it might have been a person, and, yes, that person might have been running away from the Dalton house.

Jess agreed with the police that it wasn't much, but it was more than they'd had up until now. He told Kerry this much, and no more, although their neighbor had made one other ambiguous observation: "If what I saw was a man—and mind you, I'm not saying it was—then I can tell you this: he was big! In fact, now that I think about it, it went through my mind for just a second or two that it was Pastor Dalton, since he's such a big man himself, you know. But that wouldn't make any sense, now would it, because why in the world would the pastor be running away from his own house?"

It was the comment about a "big man" that bothered Jess most. He remembered clearly Kerry's description of the man who had abducted her: "a great, hulking lout," she had called him.

Not knowing how she might react to the possibility of the man having been close to her again, Jess chose, at least for the time being, to keep it to himself. He did, however, remind the police of the similarity of the descriptions.

More afraid than ever for her safety, Jess tried to talk Kerry out of going through with the plan to spend Thanksgiving Day at the school. With a feeling bordering on shame, he admitted to himself that, if he could, he'd lock her away from the outside world entirely until this whole ordeal was resolved. Lately, it seemed that he spent most of his waking hours in fear for her. The tension was wringing him dry.

Thus he found himself faced with the undesirable choice of either reneging on his original suggestion about helping with the Thanksgiving dinner at the school or following through with it, knowing he would spend the entire day in the grip of anxiety simply because Kerry would be in an environment he couldn't control.

As was often the case in their marriage, though, she got her way. Widening her eyes in an innocent stare, she declared that since both he and Mackenzie—as well as a number of the children's fathers—would be around her all during the day, surely she'd be "adequately guarded."

The deciding factor, however, was when she twisted the knife just enough to remind him of the fact that all this had been his idea in the first place and she'd never known him to go back on his word.

Thanksgiving Day started before dawn for Molly and Kerry, and not long afterward for the men of the house.

A few minutes before seven that morning, Mackenzie made the mistake of walking into the kitchen. He grinned broadly at Adeline Corbett, who had asked to participate in the plans and was just tying the strings of a ruffled white apron around her slender waist. The caretaker went immediately to the stove and lifted the lids off various pans to inspect their contents. When no one so much as acknowledged his presence, he squared his shoulders, cleared his throat, and inquired about breakfast.

Bristling, Molly planted her hands on her hips and snapped at him fiercely enough to make him jump away with a surly growl.

"Sure and you needn't be expecting to be waited on this morning, Murtagh Mackenzie!" With one forward move, she elbowed him out of the way, pushing between him and Kerry to lift a massive kettle of potatoes onto the large iron stove. After setting the kettle carefully in place, she turned on Mackenzie and waved a large cooking spoon at him with firm orders to "do for himself!"

Jess chose that moment to enter the kitchen, earning himself a dark glare of exasperation from Molly and an amused shrug from his wife. Assessing the situation, he wisely asked if he could help.

"Indeed you can!" retorted Molly without hesitation. "We'll be needing more wood, and the trap will have to be cleaned and padded a bit before we can load all this food onto it."

"Consider it done," he answered agreeably. Thinking he had sufficiently ingratiated himself, he ventured another question. "Ah . . . will there be breakfast today, Molly?"

Without turning from the stove, where she was pouring water over the potatoes, Molly gave him a short reply. "You'll have to be doing with leftover biscuits and curd cake this morning. I put a plate of each on the dining room table along with fresh coffee."

Mackenzie lifted his chin and snarled at the housekeeper. "And why wouldn't you tell me that when I asked, woman?"

The housekeeper raised her head from the kettle of potatoes, her dark eyes flashing dangerously. Again, she waved her spoon in Mackenzie's direction with a wild swipe.

"And have I recently been taken into your employ without my knowledge, old man? Wirra!* Off with you now, the both of you!" she ordered, once more peeling the air with her spoon, this time aiming it at Jess.

Suddenly she stopped and looked down at her feet where a playful Brian Boru was stepping off the distance to one plump ankle. She shrieked, "And get that puca* out of my kitchen! Now, mind you!"

Smelling a good fight, the kitten started to circle Molly's feet, whirling faster and faster as the housekeeper turned and hopped from one foot to the other. Losing her balance, she dropped the large spoon. It clattered to the floor beside the kitten, who immediately leaped from one end of it to the other, creating a seesaw effect that obviously delighted him.

Molly's face went from amazement to fury to revenge as she classified the cat in descriptive Gaelic, relegating him to the category of disgrace formerly reserved for Oliver Cromwell, British landlords, and gombeen men*.

For a split second, Kerry thought Jess was going to fall to his knees in a fit of laughter. He looked about to strangle and was foolish enough to laugh aloud—only for an instant, though. A covert glance at Molly, who appeared to be in the throes of a seizure, quickly sobered him.

Sensible Irishman that he was, Mackenzie didn't laugh, but merely stood watching, his face expressionless, his eyes dancing with keen enjoyment. Adeline Corbett turned discreetly away so Molly couldn't see the uncontrollable smile breaking across her features.

Momentarily reluctant to end al the fun, Kerry finally decided that, in the interest of saving all nine of Brian Boru's lives, she needed to act at once. She rushed across the room, grabbed the kitten with one hand and retrieved the now contaminated spoon with the other. Flashing a quicksilver, ingenuous smile, she offered the spoon to Molly and then hurried out of the kitchen with the disappointed kitten tucked safely under her arm.

By two o'clock that afternoon, the schoolroom had taken on the appearance of a banquet hall. The tables Jess and Mackenzie had improvised from planks and logs were covered with white dinner cloths Molly and Kerry had made from old sheets. Rich, enticing odors filled the entire room, emanating from the serving tables laden with roast turkey, dressing, baked ham, potato soup, soused herring, gravy, sweet potatoes, fruit loaves, assorted pies, and half a dozen different puddings.

Kerry had all she could do to keep Jess from tasting everything in sight; Mackenzie, too, did his fair share of sneaking small samples. Molly finally took over and chased both men away with a flap of her apron and a few words of warning.

Soon the little schoolhouse was crammed snugly with children and their parents. The adult guests were obviously uncomfortable and ill at ease at first, but not for long. Kerry watched with growing relief as Jess and Mackenzie moved among the men; eventually, they were all talking and laughing comfortably.

Molly matter-of-factly went about herding everyone to the tables, occasionally enlisting the help of some of the women. Continuing to hover and fuss, she made sure everybody ate twice as much as they needed—especially, Kerry noticed with fond amusement, the children.

Adeline Corbett was the surprise of the day. Throughout the afternoon she could be found with an infant on one side of her lap and a toddler on the other. After everyone was uncomfortably sated with food, the slim, attractive widow rolled up the sleeves of her frilly white shirtwaist and trooped outside to play ball with some of the older children.

Kerry noted with interest that Mackenzie seemed more than a little fascinated with their charming neighbor. Mrs. Corbett appeared to be the focus of his attention for a large part of the afternoon. Even more interesting, though, was the disgruntled glare she caught Molly casting at Mackenzie every few moments. If I didn't know better, Kerry thought, I would be inclined to think that Molly is . . . jealous. She immediately shook off the idea, suppressing a smile at her own foolishness. To her knowledge, the housekeeper and the caretaker never so much as offered a kind word to each other. Molly, jealous? Hardly.

Late in the afternoon, Kerry went looking for Jess. She found him outside, sitting Indian style under a large willow tree with a group of small, wide-eyed boys. A mixture of affection and sadness tugged gently at her heart as she stood watching him with the children. His hair windblown and his face smudged, he looked young, relaxed, and happy in his plaid flannel shirt and the canvas pants he had rolled up above his ankles to play leapfrog and kick-the-can.

She saw he was teaching the boys to make slingshots, combining his instructions with a fast-paced, colorful account of David's slaying of Goliath. When he looked up and saw Kerry watching, he grinned and waved before returning his attention to the circle of small admirers surrounding him.

He should have had a son . . . many sons, she thought sorrowfully. Her eyes misted, and she had to walk away from the scene. Oh, dear Lord, he would have been such a wonderful father.

She stood at the edge of the school yard, staring out across the river. When she felt Jess gently rest his hands on her shoulders, she rubbed quickly at her eyes. He said nothing for a time but simply let her lean back against him.

Like a great, aging queen determined to claim her throne to the very end, the late afternoon sun hovered above the dome of the Capitol Building in a bronze and golden arc before slipping slowly out of view.

"It's lovely, isn't it?" Kerry said softly.

"Glorious," he replied, turning her around in his arms. "I've seen only one thing in my lifetime that's more lovely than a sunset." His smile left no doubt whatsoever as to his meaning.

When she didn't answer, he searched her eyes for a long moment. "What is it, dear? What's made you sad?"

"It's nothing," she murmured, unwilling to spoil the moment.

He lifted one dark brow in gentle contradiction and absently tucked a silky curl behind her ear.

She shook her head and glanced down at the ground. "I suppose it was . . . seeing you with the children, seeing how good you are with them, how they enjoy you—and how you enjoy them."

With a gentle hand, he cupped her chin and tilted her head upward to look into her eyes. "Don't, sweetheart. Don't be hurt," he said quietly. "I enjoy them, yes. But I'm not wishing for anything other than what I have."

She was unable to believe his assurance, although she wanted to with all her heart. When she would have looked away from him, he framed her face between his hands and held her gaze. "Kerry, I'm telling you the truth. I've accepted our being childless— because of you, because of the way you fill my life. Please . . . don't be sad."

His love-filled gaze went over her face with concern. "It's going to be all right, little love. I've prayed and prayed that our Lord will give you . . . something . . . to help ease the loss, to help fill the emptiness. And I believe He will."

Her eyes reflected the plea of her heart. "You truly do believe that, Jess?" she asked with a husky catch in her voice.

With great tenderness, he pressed his cheek to hers. "Yes, mavourneen,* I do," he told her softly. "As much as I love you, God loves you even more—and he's not going to let you grieve forever."

He smiled into her eyes. "Come along, now. Last I heard, Molly was insisting on a bit of music from you and Mack. And as you know, it doesn't do to keep Molly waiting."

In those first weeks of her convalescence after losing the baby, Kerry and Mackenzie had discovered a mutual love for the traditional Irish music. As soon as Kerry was able to be up and around, the caretaker shyly introduced her to his unusual collection of musical instruments—and his uncommon facility with each of them.

After learning that Kery played the flute and the fife, he took it upon himself to teach her his clairseach—a small, wire-strung folk harp which he had made himself—and the concertina. The two of them, coaxed by Jess and Molly, spent numerous evenings playing their instruments after dinner.

Today, in addition to Kerry's flute, they had brought a fiddle and a bodhran.* Mackenzie had brought his harp, too, which he played expertly in the ancient manner with his fingernails, using his left hand on the treble.

The children danced with delight, and the grown-ups stamped their feet and clapped as the two musicians regaled them with a number of traditional hornpipes, reels, and jigs. Even the few parents who had remained somewhat aloof throughout the day, as if they were unable to accept the sincerity of the Daltons' gesture of friendship, at last surrendered their reserve.

When Molly, in a rare moment of civility with Mackenzie, requested "The Minstrel Boy," everyone sat in hushed silence as the big Irishman rendered the poignant old ballad in a surprisingly clear, strong tenor.

The musicians closed the evening with a medley of the blind harper O'Carolan's tunes. As the last plaintive notes held and echoed across the room, Kerry glanced at Molly and saw that the housekeeper's eyes were clouded with tears. For one very special moment, she knew that the three of them—Molly, Mackenzie, and herself—had felt the bittersweet stirrings of a common memory, that ancient, ageless bond of the heart . . . Erin remembered.

In the middle of the night, Kerry awakened with the unpleasant awareness that she was about to pay for her over-indulgence of the day's rich food. A minor rebellion seemed to be taking place in her stomach, and when the churning failed to subside after several moments, she decided to go downstairs and get some of Molly's stomach elixir, an unpleasant thought, at best.

Molly refused to reveal the contents of the foul-tasting stuff she kept in the kitchen pantry—but it never failed to work. Kerry had suffered a number of stomach upsets lately, probably because of strain and worry, and the elixir had proven surprisingly effective.

With a reluctant sigh, she eased herself out of Jess's arms, put on her dressing gown, and lit a small candle. As she tiptoed out of the room, Brian Boru raised his head once, uttered a drowsy meow, then immediately nestled himself deeper into the plump cushion in his basket and closed his eyes.

The house was cold, and Kerry shivered as she reached the bottom of the stairs. Hurrying through the dining room into the kitchen, she bumped into a chair that had been pulled out from the table. With a muffled exclamation, she went into the pantry and rummaged through the cabinets until she found the elixir.

After swallowing two spoonsful of the mixture and drinking a small glass of milk to kill the taste of it, she retrieved her candle and left the kitchen. She got as far as the bottom of the stairway. With a puzzled frown, Kerry stopped and glanced about the reception hall, listening. As she stood there, a shroud of icy fear draped her entire body. Her heart lurched, skipped a beat, then began to bang wildly against her rib cage.

From somewhere in the cold, silent darkness came a whisper—then another. The pulse at Kerry's throat thudded even harder. Paralyzed with fear, she stared wide-eyed at the massive front door as if she expected someone to come charging through it at any moment. A dizzy feeling of approaching disaster caused her to reel slightly backward, grabbing onto the satin-smooth baluster to steady herself.

She glanced down at the candle in her hand, unable to decide whether or not she should extinguish it. Too frightened to face the total darkness of the hall, she let it be.

She heard the murmuring again, somewhat louder this time. Swallowing with great difficulty she took one cautious step forward, certain now that the sounds were outside, but close. Very close, she thought, as her heart gave another violent wrench.

Drawing in a deep, ragged breath, Kerry eyed the narrow panes of glass on either side of the front door. Fearful of being seen, she reluctantly blew out the candle, placed it on the second step from the landing, and began walking slowly toward the door.

She glanced from one side to the other with each step, moving as quietly as possible. The cold of the house mingled with the chill of her fear, and she began to tremble. The palms of her hands were wet with clammy perspiration, and she nervously wiped them on the sides of her dressing gown.

Just before she reached the door, she stopped, Perhaps I should go upstairs and call Jess . . . perhaps I should cry out for Mackenzie . . . perhaps someone is trying to break into the house and if I am simply standing here in the hall when they—

She jumped, nearly bolting from the room when she heard a cracking sound outside, followed by what sounded like the rustle of dry leaves. There was an abrupt shout, then the sound of departing hoofbeats. Quickly, she flattened herself against the wall by the door so she could peer out one narrow pane of glass.

It was a clear night, and most of the enormous old trees in the yard stood stripped of their leaves. But what foliage remained on the dense branches made it difficult to see anything but shadows.

Pressing herself even closer to the wall, Kerry craned her neck a little more. Puzzled, she stared at one of the trees closest to the house; somehow it looked different. One side appeared to be drooping from the weight of something, but it was impossible to make out what.

She glanced around the reception hall, her mouth dry, her

eyes wet with hot, nervous tears of fright. Turning her gaze back to the glass partition, she caught a glimpse of a dark, shadowy form that appeared to be moving across a corner of the yard.

She stiffened, holding her breath as she watched. The shadow stopped suddenly, then once more began to sway back and forth. She cast an uncertain glance up the stairway, then looked back to the door; finally she decided to go upstairs after Jess.

With her pulse pounding painfully in her ears, she cautiously started to back away from the door. So intent was she at remaining perfectly quiet, she failed to realize that Brian Boru was padding softly down the stairs. The kitten stopped for a curious look at the heavy brass candlestick Kerry had left on the step. He took a playful swipe at it with one paw, then another, this time knocking it over. He watched with interest as it bounced off the bottom two steps and fell to the parquet floor with a clang.

Startled by the noise, Kerry whirled around, momentarily losing her balance. At the same time, the kitten came bounding toward her, causing her to trip over him and step on his tail.

He screeched, and Kerry echoed it with a terrified scream of her own. Then, as though the sound of her voice had released a pent-up torrent of fear deep inside her, she screamed again.

Within seconds, Jess appeared at the top of the stairway, flinging on his dressing gown and rushing down the stairs. Molly appeared from her room off the kitchen, a fat beeswax candle flickering wildly in her hand. Mackenzie was no more than a moment behind her, his shillelagh raised for action.

"Kerry! What's wrong?" Out of breath and still dazed with sleep, Jess grabbed Kerry's shoulders, looking first at her, then glancing anxiously around the shadowed reception hall.

Mackenzie seemed to be everywhere at once, charging around the hall and peering into the adjoining rooms. Molly snapped angrily at the kitten, who, terrified by all the commotion, immediately ran and hid under a chair in the parlor.

Jess raised a hand to hush everyone, then turned back to Kerry, who was clutching the front of his dressing gown, her eyes round with fear.

"Jess! I heard voices—and someone was moving around outside—there's someone out there, I think—" Her words spilled from her in a tumble of meaningless gasps as she frantically tried to make herself understood.

Instantly alert, Jess clasped her firmly by the shoulders. "Kerry—slow down, love. Tell me what happened."

Kerry caught her breath, still running her words together in a hoarse whisper but now making more sense. "I came downstairs ... to get some stomach medicine . . . When I came out of the kitchen . . . I heard noises . . . outside . . . like people talking . . . then I heard horses ride off—" She stopped, swallowed, and thought for a moment. "Brian knocked the candlestick off the step, and I accidentally stepped on him . . . I screamed . . . I was coming for you, but—"

Jess pulled her tightly against himself and glanced over her head at Mackenzie with a worried frown. "Are you all right, love?" he asked, his voice tight with anxiety.

Kerry nodded against his chest, trying to drag deep breaths of air into her constricted lungs, willing herself to stop her violent trembling. "I was afraid to look out."

Again Jess's gaze met the caretaker's. "Mack, would you get a lantern?"

Mackenzie was back in an instant. When Jess gently put Kerry away from him, she started to follow the two men to the front door. Jess turned and stopped her with a firm hand on her shoulder. "No," he said flatly. "You're to stay inside with Molly." He glanced at the housekeeper, who nodded and reached out to grip Kerry by the forearm.

As soon as Jess and Mackenzie walked outside, however. Kerry pulled away from Molly and started toward the door.

"Lass, you heard—"

Ignoring her, Kerry went out the door, stepping slowly and carefully onto the porch. Molly clucked her tongue, muttering in exasperation as she followed.

Kerry watched the two men move out into the yard, Mackenzie extending the lantern slightly outward to cast enough light for both of them to see a few feet in front of them.

They walked slowly and cautiously, not speaking. When Kerry saw them come to an abrupt stop, she inched her way to the edge of the porch so she could see better.

Molly immediately moved to her side. "Let's go back inside, lass! We'll both catch our death out in this cold with no coats!"

"Shhh! They've found something!"

Quickly lifting the hem of her dressing gown, Kerry raced down the steps and hurried over to where the men were standing. Molly quietly went after her, apprehensive but curious.

Pushing herself between Jess and Mackenzie, Kerry saw nothing at first but the stunned anger on the caretaker's face and the look of astonished horror that had settled over Jess. She squinted into the shadows of the trees, her eyes focusing slowly in the dim glow cast by the lantern. Following the direction of Mackenzie's gaze as he lifted the lantern slightly higher, she instinctively stepped forward, only to be stopped by Jess's firm, almost painful grasp on her arm.

"Kerry—don't! Go back to the—"

But it was too late. Kerry saw, in brutal clarity, what Jess would have spared her. Her eyes locked on the scene in front of her, her face contorting into an image of disbelieving revulsion. As if from a great distance, she heard a shuddering roar, quickly peaking in a thundering din somewhere inside her head.

Her mind clamored to retreat, unwilling to accept the awful, hideous reality in front of her. She squeezed her eyes shut and braced herself for what she knew would still be there when she opened them again.

It was real, sickeningly, dreadfully real. She wanted to scream in denial, but she had no voice. She was dimly aware that Jess had pulled her almost roughly against him and was trying to make her turn away, but she twisted in his arms, willing herself to confront, with deadly calm, the two effigies hanging from a massive limb midway up the largest oak tree in the yard. Behind her, she heard Molly gasp. Both Jess and Mackenzie tried to lead the women away from the scene, but Kerry stood rigidly firm, as if trapped in place by some invisible force.

The larger of the two forms swinging obscenely in the night breeze, obviously intended to be Jess, wore a black clerical robe. The robe was authentic, not a facsimile. The female effigy was dressed in a plaid gown, almost identical to many of the day dresses Kerry often wore. A shawl, again similar to those Kerry

102

wore, had been tossed about its shoulders. Both faces had been crudely darkened to make them appear black, and a substance clearly meant to be blood had been splattered across the chest of each form. They dangled limply from the tree limb and swayed gently back and forth, looking incredibly, terrifyingly real.

Kerry felt her legs shake beneath her as she finally surrendered the little strength of will she had left. Numbly, she felt Jess pass her into Molly's arms. He walked over to the tree and pulled off a scrap of paper that had been fastened onto the thick trunk with a large knife.

His face paled to an ashen mask, then seemed to go slack.

"What is it, Jess?" Molly asked harshly as she continued to mindlessly pat Kerry on the back.

Jess glanced at her, then at Kerry, before looking back to the paper in his hand. "A note," he answered in a strained, rough voice. He swallowed hard, moistened his lips, and began to read in a nearly inaudible monotone:

There won't be any more warnings, Dalton. He paused a moment and looked again at Kerry. Take your Irish biddy—his voice broke for an instant before he could continue—and your darky-loving swill and get out of Washington. Or we'll carry the two of you out in matching coffins.

The last thing Kerry saw was the dark and terrible pain—or was it fear?—in Jess's eyes as he looked from her to Mackenzie, then to Molly. For an instant, she longed to go to him, to comfort him. He looks so terribly stricken, she thought, just before a softly lapping wave gently pressed her down and absorbed her into a black, peaceful pool of oblivion.

CHAPTER ELEVEN

L ate the next evening, two men faced each other across an immense, highly polished desk. The older of the two smiled coldly at the younger.

"I feel we need one more incident, just to be certain."

A small muscle at the corner of the younger man's mouth tightened, and he blinked his dark eyes nervously. "I don't think so, sir. I honestly believe he's about to quit. After last night, any rational man would give up and leave."

"I wish I could share your confidence," the man dressed in the expensively tailored suit replied. "But we're not dealing with just another hellfire-and-brimstone preacher here. Misguided as he may be, Dalton apparently believes everything he spouts from the pulpit. This man won't quit unless we push him right to the wall. And that," he said slowly with deliberate emphasis, "is exactly what I intend to do."

Pausing for only an instant, he continued in a hard, brittle voice. I don't have much time left on the Hill. Before I leave, I intend to do everything in my power to insure the rightful place of slavery in this country. We're going right to the Pacific, make no mistake about it. If the abolitionists have their way, every territory added to the United States will be prohibited from owning slaves."

Abruptly, he dropped a fist onto the top of the desk with a loud, hammering thud. "That must not happen! I'm going to stop those nigra-loving northerners if it's the last thing I do. What's the good of expanding this country if we don't have the slave labor to people its industry?"

"Senator Calhoun would say that secession is the answer," the dark-haired young man suggested hesitantly.

"Senator Calhoun is a fool." The composed, intelligent face familiar to the public was now distorted and flushed with anger. "Destroying the union will only destroy the country. That's not the way."

Something savage and not entirely sane flared in his gaze, then disappeared. With noticeable effort, he calmed himself, smoothing the lapels of his suitcoat and checking his gold watch. "The other thing I intend to do is to get this country's deplorable immigration laws drastically tightened. At the rate we're bringing in the paddys and the rest of the foreigners, our labor structure is going to collapse totally within five years—ridiculous!"

The man across from him remained silent, accustomed to being used as a sounding board.

"Dalton's trying to wangle an invitation to address the Senate, you know," the man continued in an ugly tone. "And he'll most likely get it, if I know that bunch of milksops!"

He rose from his chair, again pounding his fist on the desk. "I'm telling you, I want that rabble-rousing demagogue out of Washington! Do you understand? I want him out of this town." Seeing the surprised, somewhat speculative gaze of the younger man, he sat down abruptly, his agitation quickly replaced by an expression of impassive calm.

"It's not that I disagree with you, sir," the younger man finally spoke up. "But I can't help wondering how far we can go without all of us landing in trouble."

"Perhaps," the middle-aged man said with an edge of menace, "I need to remind you that you're not in a position to wonder about anything. Unless you want to spend the rest of your life hanging onto someone else's coattails, you'll do exactly as you're told. You have no choice—remember?"

The flash of anger in the younger man's eyes lasted only an instant before he paled and gained control of himself. "What exactly are your instructions for the others, then?" he asked tightly. "What should I tell them?"

The older man stroked his clean-shaven chin thoughtfully. "Tell them," he said in a chilling tone, "to go after the woman again. I don't want anything to happen to her, mind," he warned. "There's always the danger of driving Dalton too far and making him turn and fight—especially if he has nothing to lose. I detest the man, but I'd never make the mistake of underestimating him. Tell them to just . . . push the woman around a little. Perhaps give her a few bruises. That shouldn't be any problem," he drawled with a smile that made the younger man cringe. "They seem to enjoy their work immensely."

CHAPTER TWELVE

I don't want you to go to the school today, love. In fact, I'm asking you not to leave the house."

Surprised by Jess's remark, Kerry frowned and propped herself up against the pillows on their bed.

"But I must. I promised Cely. We have to clean the school and ready the desks and put the supplies back in order before Monday, and—"

"I'll send a message to her and explain what happened," he said, glancing at her in the mirror as he buttoned the top button of his shirt.

He turned and went to sit beside her on the bed, extending one arm at a time for her to button his sleeves. She said nothing until she had finished and he had kissed her lightly on the cheek.

"Jess, please don't ask me to stay home today. That was two days ago. I rested all yesterday, just as you asked. But I'm fine now, truly I am." She laid one hand on his forearm. "I need to go, Jess. I need to be busy. I simply can't sit around here all day and think about . . . everything."

He avoided her eyes and pretended to straighten the quilt

about her waist. "Surely you can keep busy here. And Molly and Mack are here to talk with—"

She stopped his words by framing his face with both hands and pulling his head down to hers. "You're afraid for me, and that's the truth of it, isn't it?"

When he didn't answer, she moved even closer to him, forcing him to look at her. "Don't you see, Jess, that I'm even more worried for you?"

She pressed a finger to his lips to stop his protest. "It's you, after all, they're trying to intimidate. But I haven't asked you even once to lock yourself up inside the house and not go out, now have I?"

"No, but—"

"Because I know you won't—you can't. If you insist, though, you know I'll do as you ask. But I need to go about living, too, Jess—just as you do. I can't face day after day of shutting myself away from the world. There's so little I can do to help with your work, but the school—that's one thing I can do. Please don't ask me to give it up. I need it now more than ever."

"I'm not asking you to give it up," he protested quickly.

"Aren't you, now? And what about next week, Jess?" she asked him directly. "Won't you be wanting me to stay home then as well?"

"I'm—" He couldn't deny the truth of her words. "Kerry, I'm frightened—not for myself. For you. You've been a . . . target in this whole nightmarish assault from the beginning. Don't you understand?" A desperate plea brimmed in his gaze. "I can't even bear to think about something happening to you. I can't risk your being hurt any more than you already have been."

Gently, she coaxed his head onto her shoulder and combed the springy waves of his hair with her fingers. "I do understand, avourneen* . . . aye, I do. But you must understand my feelings as well. Besides—what can happen? Mackenzie will take me to the school and come back for me, just as he always does. No one would expect Cely and me to be there today since school's not in session."

He raised his head and searched her eyes. His expression was somber, fear-edged, but resigned. "If it's that important to you, I won't ask you not to go."

"It is that important to me, Jess. But not so much that I'd see you hurt to have my way."

Kerry was almost ready to give in to his wishes, he looked so forlorn, exhausted, worried. *And he looks so much older*, she thought with a sudden stab of concern. *All this worry . . . and fear. It's done terrible things to him . . . and it just keeps happening, as though there will never be an end to it.*

"Jess—"

"Kerry, I—"

They looked at each other, waiting. Jess gave her a rueful smile and said with resignation, "It's all right; I suppose I understand. Just . . . don't stay very long?"

She hugged him hard, "I promise. I'll probably be home long before you are."

"See that you are, little missus," he said softly, studying her dear, elfin face. "I confess that I like coming home to find a beautiful lass waiting for me."

"Thank you, dearest . . . for understanding," she said fervently, kissing him long and with aching tenderness.

By ten that morning, Kerry had dressed in one of her older, somewhat worn gowns—one she thought of as a work dress. She was tucking her hair back with combs when she heard Molly's voice loud and angry from the reception hall.

With a puzzled frown, she opened her bedroom door and stepped into the hallway to see what was going on downstairs. When she reached the upstairs banister, she stopped dead, stunned to see Lowell Martin standing at the threshold of the open front door. Molly, her feet planted slightly apart and her hands braced firmly on her wide hips, was facing him.

"What nerve you have showing up at the front door of this home after your abysmal behavior!" The housekeeper made no effort to gentle her tone. Obviously infuriated with the young man at the door, she continued to rail at him, her brogue thickened by fury.

Kerry stared in astonishment as the impeccably dressed Martin twisted his mouth scornfully and silenced the housekeeper with a sharp retort.

"Remember your place, woman! Just give me a civil answer to my question and none of your sass."

Burning with anger, Kerry crossed the upstairs hall and raced down the steps to confront the tall, cold-faced man in the doorway.

Ignoring Molly's grasp on her arm as she pushed up beside her, Kerry snapped, "What are you doing here? What do you want?"

The ill-concealed contempt in Martin's raking gaze made Kerry even more furious.

"Mrs. Dalton—" his voice was smoothly correct, though Kerry could sense the scorn in his tone. "Senator Forbrush asked that I call to convey his regrets and those of the members of his household about what happened here Thanksgiving evening." He smiled ingenuously. "May I add that I, too, was outraged when I heard about the, ah . . . incident . . . that occurred on your front lawn. It must have been . . . most distressing . . . for you and the pastor."

Kerry knew he was boldly challenging her to doubt his sincerity. Hearing Molly's furious indrawn breath, she reached out a restraining hand and placed it on the housekeeper's plump forearm.

"Thank you very much, Mr. Martin," she said coldly. "I shall convey the senator's message to my husband."

Martin situated himself a few inches further inside the doorway before Molly could block him. "I wonder, Mrs. Dalton, if it would be possible for me to speak with your husband for a moment?"

"No, it would not," Kerry replied without explanation.

"I see. He's . . . out for the morning?"

Kerry nodded curtly. "If that's all—"

"Yes, of course," Martin slurred with forced politeness, glancing over his shoulder as Mackenzie brought the carriage to a halt out front. "I see you're preparing to leave. I shouldn't detain you any longer. Thank you for . . . receiving me so graciously, Mrs. Dalton." He smoothed the velvet collar on his coat, then stepped outside on the porch and lifted his gray top hat to his head. With a courteous nod to Kerry, he swaggered down the walkway, ignoring Mackenzie's narrow-eyed stare as he passed the carriage.

"Evil's own, that one!" Molly hissed. "You should have let me

112

put Mackenzie on him with his shillelagh!"

Kerry shook her head. "I wonder what he really wanted," she murmured uneasily.

Later that afternoon, Kerry plopped down onto the teacher's chair in the schoolroom and moaned with fatigue. "I'm thinking we should have recruited some men to help us, after all." Her hair had long since escaped its combs and fell in an unruly toss of tangled curls. Smudges of dust dotted her cheeks, and a spot of ink darkened one sleeve of her dress.

Cely glanced over at her from where she was shoving a box of wood onto the fireplace hearth. "You look like a little rag doll that's lost some of her stuffing," she remarked with an affectionate chuckle.

Kerry grunted and held her hands out in front of her for inspection. "Sure and wouldn't Mrs. Northcote crack her long nose if she were to see me now?"

"Well, at least we're ready for Monday." Cely rubbed her hands on both sides of her dress and cast a pleased look about the schoolroom. "I can't thank you enough for helping me with all this, Kerry. I'd have worked all weekend without you. Our new arrangement looks much better, don't you think? There's more room this way.

Kerry managed a weary nod. "Jess said the window glass will be put in before Christmas; did I tell you?"

"That soon?" Cely ran a slender hand through her short hair and stretched her arms about her head with a groan. "That going to keep this place a lot warmer." She paused a moment, then added, "You and the pastor have helped us a lot, Kerry. I'm really grateful—and so are the parents."

"Well, now, you can thank Jess and Mackenzie for most of the ideas. Seems that one or the other of them is always coming up with something new."

"Mm. And then seeing that it gets done. There have been some real improvements this year, thanks to you and—" Cely broke off in midsentence, turning to glance toward the door. "I think I hear Mackenzie with your buggy."

Kerry hauled herself to her feet, sighing with the effort. She walked over to the door and bent to pick up a bucket of water and dirty cleaning cloths. "I'll empty this before I leave, and I'll see if Mackenzie will fix that broken leg on your desk before we go."

Kerry stuck her head out the doorway to look for Mackenzie. When she didn't see him, she went on outside and down the steps to the schoolyard.

After dumping the water and wringing out the rags, she put the bucket by the steps and walked around to the back of the building, thinking Mackenzie might have come that way to avoid the deep, treacherous ruts in front.

The afternoon was mild for late November, though it was as dark as early evening. The ground was spongy from the rain they'd had earlier in the week, and the low-hanging clouds promised more rain by nightfall.

Carefully sidestepping a number of deep pits in the yard, Kerry was surprised to find that Mackenzie wasn't there either; she wondered what Cely had heard. With a shrug, she turned and started back toward the front of the building.

When she first heard the sound of men's laughter, she thought perhaps some of the children's parents had come by. When she reached the front, however, and saw the riderless horses and Cely surrounded by a group of men in the open schoolyard, she felt her heart plummet with sick fear.

At first, they didn't see her. She put a hand up against the side of the building to steady herself, her mind reeling with panicked confusion. She desperately tried to think what to do. Four white men had Cely trapped and were circling her like predators, mocking her with suggestive remarks and obscenities.

Even from a distance, Kerry could see the fury in Cely's eyes and knew she wasn't about to cower to her tormentors. The tall black woman appeared to be rigid with anger, her chin thrust defiantly upward from the long slender lines of her neck, her shoulders square and straight.

"Whooee—she's a fiery one, ain't she?"

The voice belonged to a short, porcine man with a filthy shirt and vest. He was prodding Cely's abdomen with the barrel of his rifle.

"Ever see a savage that wasn't wild?" jeered a taller man behind him who was eyeing Cely with a look that held a frightening combination of contempt and lust.

114

Kerry felt her legs tremble and her mouth go dry with fear. She could almost feel the touch of the rifle herself as Cely tried to back away from the fat man, who only punched the gun that much harder into her midle.

She swallowed and clawed the wooden frame of the building, praying silently.

The large, burly man farthest away from her caught her attention—something about his head—his large, oddly shaped head and crooked, flattened nose.

"Merciful, Lord," she whispered in horrified disbelief.

It was him! The man who had abducted her that terrible day when she first arrived in Washington. There couldn't possibly be two faces so deformed, so wretchedly revolting, in the same city.

At the sound of her gasp, the dull-witted man saw her and shrieked. "There she is! That's her!"

Every gaze turned to Kerry. Cely whirled around and shouted, "Run, Kerry!"

No one spoke for an endless moment. Kerry could feel herself paling under their mocking gazes. She couldn't run—she wouldn't leave Cely alone with them, even if there had been somewhere to go. Where was Mackenzie? He should be here by now . . .

Suddenly, the man closest to her, a thin, hard-looking man with black hair and peculiar silver eyes, moved to grab her arm. He yanked her away from the building and twisted her arm behind her so forcefully she cried out in pain.

The man shoved her against Cely, who immediately linked her hand with Kerry's. The fat man who had been goading Cely now turned his attention to Kerry, prodding her like an animal with the tip of his rifle.

To her horror, the dim-witted giant lumbered up and pulled furiously at her hair. "You hurt me! You hurt me and ran away!"

"Leave her alone!" Cely tried to protect Kerry by pushing in front of her, but, tall as she was, she was still no match for the hulking lout. It took no more than a quick jerk of his hand to tear her away from Kerry and send her sprawling to the ground.

When he turned back to Kerry, his face was scarlet with bewildered rage. "Why did you run away from me? I was supposed to take care of you!"

115

Kerry pushed a fist against her mouth to keep from crying out, unwilling to give these animals the satisfaction of seeing her terror.

"That's all right, Otis." The thin man with the odd silver eyes held the giant back with a firm hand. "She won't run away this time."

His voice was laced with mockery, his eyes cold with disdain as he flicked a glance over Kerry. "We have a message for you, Mrs. Dalton," he sneered. "And I'd advise you to listen to it very carefully."

Kerry's eyes blazed with incredulous anger and rising fear. She tried to go to Cely but was stopped by the large, beefy hand of the one called Otis.

The other two men stepped in closer and looked Kerry up and down with burning glints in their eyes that made Kerry's stomach churn with nausea. For an instant, she thought her legs would buckle under her.

The lanky, dark-haired man, who seemed to be the leader of the group, snapped her chin roughly upward and forced her to look directly at him. "Now pay attention, ma'am," he drawled contemptuously. "What we want you to do is to convince your nigra-loving husband that he has nothing more to say to the good people here in Washington. We figure he might be more inclined to listen to you than us—especially," his eyes narrowed in a nasty, threatening stare, "if we mess up your pretty little face just enough to let him know we mean business."

Kerry's blood froze at the raw evil she encountered in his eyes. Desperately, she struck out at him with her free hand, trying to twist away from his grasp. But he swiftly moved behind her and locked his arms around her waist, holding her in an iron vise.

"Let us help convince her, chief." The fat man sidled up in front of Kerry and, with absolutely no warning, he snaked out his hand and slapped her in the face.

Kerry gasped, her head reeling as much from the shock of being struck for the first time in her life as from the pain of the blow. From the ground, Cely cried out with furious protest and tried to scramble to her feet. But the hulking, disfigured Otis stopped her with a hard kick in the side from his enormous, boot-clad foot.

A young blond-haired man—in truth, he looked to be no more than a boy—stepped from behind the chief and sauntered up to Kerry. Until now, he had been silent, but Kerry saw with sick hopelessness that his eyes held nothing but malice and contempt.

"Don't be so hard on little Brigit, Sam," he said in an oily tone of voice, his gaze raking over Kerry with bold interest. "From what I hear, these Irish colleens don't understand rough stuff. They like to be sweet-talked. Isn't that right, Brigit?"

With a terrible smile, he tugged Kerry out of the chief's grasp and pulled her roughly to him, forcing his face down to hers in a crude kiss.

Kerry cried out, twisting away from him and wiping at her mouth with revulsion. He grabbed her again, this time passing her to the fat man with the offensive body odor. He, too, made a smacking motion against her face with his lips, laughing loudly when Kerry tried to rub away the foul taste of him from her mouth.

They continued to pass her back and forth, taunting her and handling her. The thin leader had no part in it but simply stood and watched with a cold, impassive stare.

So involved were they with their fun they failed to notice the carriage which pulled up in front of the school. Nor did they see the two large men jump from it—not until both were almost upon them.

They all whirled around, staring in surprise as Jess roared with rage and hurled himself into their midst. At the same time, Mackenzie plowed his way into the huddle and cracked Otis's shoulder with a hard whack of his shillelagh. Bellowing with pain, the giant charged the Irishman with his head. In spite of his advanced years, however, the caretaker was more agile—and far more alert—than the mentally impaired Otis. He deftly stepped aside to avoid him, then whacked him once more, this time in the abdomen, sending him screaming to the ground. Immediately, he moved to help Jess, who had flattened the blond youngster against the side of the schoolhouse and was reaching for the porcine Sam with his free hand. Mackenzie snarled, charged the fat man with his shillelagh, and easily knocked him off balance into the mud.

A sudden gunshot exploded, stopping them where they were. The man called the chief held a rifle on Kerry while glancing coldly from Jess to Mackenzie. "Let my men go, Dalton—now! Or you can watch me make Irish stew out of your woman."

Jess stood unmoving, still holding onto the stunned, fair-haired boy. He looked from the man with the rifle to Kerry, then to Mackenzie, whose shoulders slumped in defeat as he reluctantly let go of the fat man. Slowly, Jess released his grasp on the boy, allowing him to slide free.

Kerry had never seen hatred in her husband's eyes—but she saw it now. Hatred and a dark, terrible fury. Please, Lord, don't let him do anything foolish. Don't let him be hurt . . . oh, merciful Father, won't you please, please stop this!

Suddenly, another shot roared out in the schoolyard. All eyes turned to the form standing in the open doorway of the building. In the chaos of the moment, Cely had been forgotten. She now stood, tall and determined, a shotgun braced and aimed at the chief.

"Put it down." The command was ordered in a surprisingly calm tone of voice, while at the same time her eyes blazed with almost tangible rage.

The thin black-haired man aimed a speculative look at Cely, not moving his rifle even a fraction.

"I said put it down!"

With a look of pure menace, he lowered the rifle slowly and reluctantly, then dropped it to the ground in defeat.

Cely then turned the shotgun onto the fat man and the boy. "Move over by your boss," she instructed with a curt movement of her head.

They went without hesitation. She glanced for only an instant at Otis, still writhing in pain on the ground, then returned her attention to the other three men bunched closely together.

"What shall I do with them, Mr. Dalton?"

Jess hesitated, a question in his eyes.

She met his gaze and said dryly, "Oh, yes, Preacher—I know how to use it."

Jess still remained silent. Finally, with a look of reluctance, he shook his head and raised one hand in a gesture of restraint. "Keep them covered."

He moved quickly to Kerry, who was now hugging herself tightly, swaying back and forth as if she were trying to keep from crumbling into pieces.

"Kerry . . . are you all right?" he asked softly.

When she didn't answer, he felt a prickling of alarm. Gently, he gathered her into his arms and sheltered her closely against him, never taking his gaze from the men a few feet away. Feeling the violent trembling of her body, he held her even tighter.

"Mack—get that rifle," he said evenly, glancing down at Kerry in his arms. "Cely—bring me your gun. Mack and I will keep them here while you take the carriage and go for the police." He looked down at Kerry again, feeling his throat tighten at the way she was shaking in his arms. He wrapped her protectively against his side, extending his free hand to Cely.

Without blinking an eye, Cely walked calmly across the yard and handed Jess the shotgun. She paused only long enough to put a comforting hand on Kerry's shoulder and murmur something to her before going to the carriage.

It was midnight before Kerry finally cried. Jess had waited and worried while Molly bathed her silent mistress and helped her into a warm nightdress and bathrobe. Then, sitting down in the broad rocking chair by the fireplace in their bedroom, he pulled her onto his lap and began to talk to her in soft, gentle words of reassurance. He left her only once, to lay a fire and make certain it would burn for a while.

She trembled in his arms a long time, not speaking, not even looking at him. Finally, his loving tenderness penetrated her shock, and he felt her slender shoulders rise and fall as she began to shake uncontrollably with violent sobs.

Her hand clutched at his shirtfront, and he covered it gently with his own. "That's right, little love, you cry," he murmured into her hair. "Cry out all the ugliness, my darling. Cry it all away."

Throughout the long, silent hours of the seemingly endless night, Jess held Kerry in his lap like a small, grieving child. He rocked her slowly back and forth in the quiet warmth of their room, holding her close, humming songs without meaning, melodies without words. He listened to her hopeless sobs weaken, then finally cease. Even when she finally slept, he continued rocking and humming softly, as if he were determined to insure her peace, at least for a few hours.

Occasionally, he brushed a damp wave of hair away from her face or touched his lips gently to her temple. Sometimes, he simply looked at her and let his heart fill and overflow with love.

His shirt was wet from her tears, and his eyes were tired and scratchy from his own weeping; his thoughts were weary and confused. Why hadn't he taken her from this place before now? So much loss . . . so much suffering. Why had he even come? He had accomplished nothing.

The town is a wasteland, he decided bitterly. On the surface it buzzes and clamors with important plans and activity, but its heart . . . its heart is desperate and uncaring, even ruthless. People are sacrificed for politics, and justice is exchanged for power. Nothing is allowed to stop the ambition of a few . . . nothing is sacred.

Kerry moaned softly and burrowed deeper into the hollow of his shoulder. He felt the warmth of her even breathing against the pulse at his throat and he smiled, lightly resting his chin on top of her head so he could enjoy the sweet fragrance of her hair; he continued to rock and hum and cherish her.

I love her so, Lord. I love her so much it's a wonder my heart doesn't explode with it.

He raised his head enough to press a gentle kiss into the cloud of her hair, then resumed his prayer.

We've come to a crossing, haven't we, Father? I have to decide exactly what to do, where to go from here. And I can't be long in making up my mind. Too much is at stake. Oh, Lord, please speak to my spirit tonight. Give me at least enough of your wisdom, your guidance, to help me see what I'm to do about all this. And give me a way to keep my beloved safe and out of the reach of this evil. Please, Lord, keep her from any more pain. She's already been hurt so much because of me. Please—let it end. Let it end before it breaks her . . . before it destroys us.

Save us, Lord, I beg you. Save the both of us.

CHAPTER THIRTEEN

By the next morning, Jess knew what he had to do; he also knew that Kerry would oppose him. Somehow, he would have to convince her that it was the only way.

Through the long dark hours of the night, he had considered every available alternative. The most drastic resolution, of course, would be to simply uproot his household and leave Washington. As soon as the idea entered his mind, however, he knew he couldn't possibly do it. In spite of all the problems and resistance he had encountered, he still had the responsibility of ministering to his congregation. At present, he was sure of very little, but he was certain it wasn't the Lord's will for him to desert the people he had promised to shepherd.

In addition, the invitation he'd hoped for from the Senate had arrived at the church only hours before the terrorizing incident at the school; he now had permission to address the Senate, as early as next week if he wanted. He had prayed for this opportunity for a long time; should he now turn his back on it?

If he were to ask for a temporary leave of absence from his pastorate—a few weeks—to take Kerry and Molly away and get them safely settled elsewhere before he returned, where exactly would he take them? Besides, what would it accomplish?

Finally, his eyes aching and his heart heavy, he wrote a letter which he intended to dispatch as soon as he talked with Kerry after the morning's worship service.

She was still sleeping when he left the house, and he gave Molly instructions not to wake her. "I hate to ask you to miss Sunday worship, Molly, but if you would stay—"

"Never you fret about that, Jess. I'd not be able to keep my mind on the service anyway," the housekeeper quickly assured him.

Mackenzie insisted upon driving Jess to the church. A strong north wind with an accompanying sharp drop in temperature had stormed through the city in the predawn hours, and it was now bitterly cold. The caretaker returned home as soon as he left Jess, telling him he'd be back with the carriage later. Like Molly, Mackenzie was anxious about the little missus and chose to stay close to her that day.

After the service was over and Jess had greeted what he believed to be the last of the Sunday worshipers, he walked back into the sanctuary. He stopped in midstride when he saw Senator Calhoun, his wife, and his aide standing close to the pew where they had been seated earlier.

Jess had been surprised to see the famous southerner at the service that day. After the dramatic exit of the politicians and their families the week before, he had expected the withdrawals of several memberships. And, indeed, the Northcotes had done exactly that. Having had no word from the Calhouns or Preston Forbrush, he still did not expect to see either of them again. Now, it seemed that the tall, thin senator was obviously waiting for him.

Although he was aging, Calhoun was still a powerful, intimidating man in appearance and manner. As Jess walked up to the senator, it occurred to him that, had the two of them not been at such extreme odds politically, he would have greatly enjoyed Calhoun's friendship. He had long admired the man's strength of character and political brilliance.

"Senator?" Jess stopped and waited, wondering uncomfortably what to expect.

The older man said nothing for a moment but simply stared at Jess through measuring eyes. When he spoke, it was with some degree of awkwardness.

"Mr. Dalton—I want to express my regrets about the . . . incident involving your wife at the nigra school yesterday," he said stiffly.

Surprised that Calhoun even knew anything about the incident, Jess was even more astonished at his words. "Well . . . thank you, Senator. Certainly, I appreciate your concern."

The tall, somewhat waspish South Carolinian pulled his heavy gray brows together in a frown. "There's something I want to say to you, sir. While I find your northern ties and your antislavery sympathies insufferable, I view what happened to Mrs. Dalton as an unforgivable outrage, a most regrettable experience. I want you to know that if I can help you discover who was behind that crowd of low-life rowdies, I shall be happy to do so."

Stunned by the senator's words, Jess almost failed to express his gratitude.

Calhoun started to move away, then stopped. "Have the police been able to get any information out of those thugs yet?"

Jess shook his head. "No—nothing. One of the investigating officers stopped here at the church earlier this morning. He said not a one of them would talk."

The senator thinned his mouth to a hard line. "Bad business, this. No one but a coward would attack a woman to gain his own ends." He stopped abruptly, glanced around as if embarrassed by his offer of assistance, then motioned to his wife and aide.

"Senator Calhoun—" Jess hesitated.

The older man turned and waited.

"I . . . thank you, sir. I'll convey your concern to my wife."

Calhoun nodded, squared his shoulders, lifted his chin, and marched out of the sanctuary, his wife and aide hurrying along beside him.

That afternoon, their usual large and sumptuous Sunday dinner was mostly a wasted effort on Molly's part. Kerry ate virtually nothing, and Jess was indifferent at best, though cherry-glazed baked ham was one of his favorites.

Molly shook her head and clucked softly to herself, uncommonly subdued as she removed their pie plates, each still holding a large wedge of uneaten custard pie. The housekeeper, sensing the tension in the room, worked quietly. Once the table had been cleared and she'd brought them fresh coffee, she immediately left Jess and Kerry alone.

"You scarcely touched your meal, love," Jess said softly, reaching across the table to take her hand gently in his.

"Nor did you." Kerry stirred her coffee distractedly and stared down at the table. "How did this morning's service go?"

"Very well. I had a surprise, though. Senator Calhoun and his wife were there."

She glanced up. "You thought they wouldn't be back, didn't you?"

"I was afraid they might withdraw their membership along with the Northcotes, yes," he admitted. "Even more astonishing, they waited for me afterward—to deliver a message."

"A message? What sort of message?"

She looked surprised but pleased when he repeated Calhoun's words. "I was caught so unaware I'm afraid I barely responded." Rising from his chair, he came around the table to sit down beside her, bringing his coffee with him.

"We must talk, love," he said after lowering himself into the chair. "There are decisions that we have to make."

She searched his eyes, her gaze at first questioning, then wary. "What sory of decisions, Jess?"

"Kerry . . ." He knew he must be very careful of how he raised the subject. "I'm going to ask you to do something for me, something I'm afraid you won't like very well."

She sat quietly, studying his face with a worried look.

He drew in a steadying breath. "I want you to understand that if I could think of another solution, I would never suggest what I'm about to say. But—we have to do something, and I truly don't know what else to do."

She waited, saying nothing.

"Kerry, I've written to my Aunt Marian in New York—my mother's sister. I've told you about her, remember? I've asked her if you can stay with her for a short time."

124

"Stay with her?" Her expression was blank, uncomprehending.

"Yes, love. I . . . I want you to leave Washington . . . for now—just until I can find out who's responsible for this . . . attack that's been mounted against us. And until I can . . . perhaps locate another pastorate."

He avoided her gaze, although he knew her eyes were burning into him.

The room was silent for a long moment. Then, slowly and distinctly, as though in a daze, Kerry said, "You want me to leave?

He heard the note of disbelieving hurt in her voice and immediately reached for her hand, forcing himself to meet the pain in her eyes. "Don't say it like that, Kerry. Of course I don't want you to leave. But . . . I don't know what else to do."

She jerked her hand away and drew back as sharply as if he'd struck her. "I won't!" She continued to stare at him incredulously. "Don't even think it."

"Kerry—" He reached for both her hands and clasped them securely in his. "Listen to me—please. We have to do something. We can't continue to live like this."

She shook her head in stubborn denial. "No—No! I won't listen to you. Not for a moment."

The vehemence in her voice made Jess realize that, if anything, he'd underestimated the intensity of her reaction.

"Love of my heart . . ."

"Don't!" She was close to shouting at him, and her eyes were on fire with anger and unshed tears. "Don't you dare do this with me, Jess Dalton! Don't you dare to be talking to me as if I'm a child! I'll not listen to you—I won't!"

She yanked her hands roughly out of his grasp and started to rise. Jess caught her, gently but firmly, and pressed her back onto the chair.

"You must listen to me, Kerry. I'm only talking about a short time, two or three weeks at most."

She sat down reluctantly, her eyes fixing him with a wounded, accusing glare.

"I just want to get you . . . out of harm's way, love, long enough to make some decisions—long enough to address the Senate."

At her look of surprise, he nodded. "The invitation came

125

yesterday morning. That's why I was with Mack when he came for you at the school," he explained. "I couldn't wait to tell you, and when I got home and you weren't here, I decided to come along with Mack to pick you up." He glanced away from her for a moment, then added softly, "Thank the Lord I did come with him."

Her look softened only a little, but she allowed him to again envelop both her hands within his. "I'm glad for you, Jess—about the Senate address," she murmured, lowering her eyes.

"Kerry . . . beloved . . . please try to understand. I can't think straight any longer," he said hoarsely. "I'm so afraid for you, so terrified that something awful is going to happen to you . . . because of me. I'm losing all sense of reason. I'm afraid for you to leave the house—and afraid for you to stay at home." He released one hand and raked it almost savagely through his hair. "Once I know you're safe . . . perhaps I can function rationally again."

He pulled her close to him and locked his eyes with hers. "Kerry . . . please do this for me. I swear to you, if the police don't get to the bottom of all this madness and do something about it within three weeks, I'll leave my pastorate here. That will give me time to appear in front of the Senate, time to make some plans for us. Three weeks, Kerry," he promised again. "One way or another I'll come for you by then. If things are no better here, we'll go back to the Academy, if they'll have me, or somewhere else—anywhere besides Washington. I promise you, love."

Closing her eyes against the scalding tears fighting to break free, Kerry drew a long breath of despair.

"I don't want you to quit, Jess—not because of me."

"If I quit," he said bitterly. "it won't be because of you. It will be because of a group of unscrupulous madmen."

"Jess . . ." Her eyes clouded with dismay. "I don't want to leave you. Please don't ask me to do this." She hurried on when he would have protested. "Oh, I'm afraid sometimes, I can't pretend I'm not. Mostly I'm afraid for you, though. You were so sure our Lord called you to this place, that you were led here. It's for me to stand with you now, don't you see?"

"Kerry—" He wiped at his red-rimmed eyes with the back of

one hand, a tired gesture of frustration. "You don't understand what I'm thinking, what I—"

"I believe I do," she interrupted quietly. "You're thinking that you must quit, or I'll be hurt. You're basing your entire decision on me."

He stared at her, unable to deny her accusation. "I cannot . . . continue to exercise my own stubborn beliefs at your expense," he said, his voice rough with emotion. "I love you too much for that."

"Jess, avourneen* . . ." Kerry gently framed his face between her hands and searched his gaze for a long time; neither of them spoke. It was the worry, the fine lines of fatigue and shadows around his eyes that finally made her lose her resolve to defy him. "Will it truly help you—if I do what you're asking? Is this really what you want?"

He attempted to memorize every line, every contour of her beloved face. "It will tear my heart out," he said softly. "But, yes . . . it's what I need you to do."

"Then . . . I'll go, Jess," she choked out. "If that's the only way . . . of course, I'll go."

Slowly, he rose from his chair and pulled her to her feet with him, wrapping her in his arms in a protective embrace.

"Molly will go with you."

"No!" She drew back and frowned at him with concern. "Molly must stay with you. I'll only worry myself sick if you're alone here with no one to do for you."

"Kerry, I'm capable of doing for myself, love," he insisted, attempting a weak laugh. "And Mack will be here, as well."

"No, Jess!" She gave a brusque, determined shake of her head. "Molly must stay with you. I won't go otherwise."

With a rueful smile, he gave in. "All right—all right, if it will make you feel better." He gathered her more closely against himself and dropped a light kiss on top of her head, wondering silently how he would every survive the coming weeks without her.

"If you won't let me send Molly, I'm going to ask Charles to accompany you to New York and see you safely to my aunt's home."

Surprised, she protested. "You can't be without your secretary.

127

Besides, it's entirely unnecessary."

"It is necessary, love, for my peace of mind. I won't rest until I know for certain that you've been safely delivered into Aunt Marian's care. Charles is a bit awkward and difficult to be with, I know. But he's a good lad, and I've talked with him from time to time about what's been done to us. I'm sure he'll be glad to escort you."

He hesitated, then added, "I'd take you myself, but I have both the Caldwell wedding and the Senate address this week—"

She waved a dismissing hand. "You can't possibly leave now. And if you're determined that I need someone with me, then I've no objection to Charles Payne. But I think you're being a bit foolish."

"When haven't I been a bit foolish, little love, where you're concerned?" he murmured, kissing her tenderly on her forehead. Oh, Kerry, Kerry, love of my heart . . . how will I ever get through my days without your smile, without your touch . . . our love?

CHAPTER FOURTEEN

Kerry's good-bye to Molly and Mackenzie a few days later was a tearful prelude to her agonizing parting with Jess.

"You're doing the right thing, lass," sniffed the housekeeper. Molly had obviously been crying earlier; her face was puffy, her eyes swollen. She patted Kerry awkwardly on the shoulder, avoiding her gaze. "It's best, lass. I know you're heartsore—aren't we all. But something had to be done. It will be all right soon, see if it's not."

Mackenzie stood silently, staring down at the scuffed toes of his boots and holding a squirming Brian Boru close to his chest. Kerry stroked the kitten under his chin, biting furiously at her lower lip in an attempt to stifle a sob of pain. She looked up into Mackenzie's mournful face, then impulsively threw her arms around his neck and kissed him on his grizzled cheek. The big Irishman wiped one hand over his eyes in a hasty motion and muttered, "We'll be missing you something fierce, missus."

Kerry heard the choked catch in his voice. Oddly enough, the apparent grief of these two devoted friends supplied her with the

129

needed incentive to pull her own emotions together. She lifted her head firmly and managed a smile for both of them.

"You'll take very good care of our Jess?"

"We'll see to him as best we can, you can be sure of that," Molly said, fighting to regain her composure.

"Aye, that we will," Mackenzie echoed. He hesitated a moment then added gruffly, "We'll keep him safe and well for you, little missus. You're not to fret yourself about that."

"And Brian Boru as well?" she asked softly, casting an appealing look at Molly.

The housekeeper's lip quivered slightly, then she nodded. "He'll not be without proper feeding and a bit of attention, lass, rest your mind."

Giving each of them one last embrace, Kerry turned and fled down the walk to the carriage where Jess and Charles Payne waited for her.

They said little on the way to the train station. Charles drove the carriage while Jess kept one arm around Kerry, watching her out of the corner of his eye. She sat stiffly erect, clutching his hand tightly and looking straight ahead.

With a sick heaviness of heart, he wondered if she were afraid, knowing she would try to conceal it if she were. In her customary concern for him, she would attempt to make this day as easy as possible. Always, she put him first. Dear little love . . . I am strangling with grief even as I sit here beside you. How can I possibly let you board that train? How can I bring myself to let you go?

The shy, dark-haired secretary was swift to leave them alone when they reached the station, offering to see to Kerry's luggage so they could say their good-byes in private.

The few moments they had together before she had to board seemed to fly. All too soon, she was clinging to Jess to avoid the final, wrenching farewell.

"You must go, love—it's time," he murmured into the soft fragrance of her hair, making no move to release her from his embrace.

She nodded, locking her arms around his neck even tighter. "Jess . . ." Her voice broke, and she finished her question in a whisper. ". . . You're sure . . . that I must do this?"

He felt his shoulders heave, his heart sink, and he knew he was about to lose what little control he had left.

"Kerry . . . sweet . . . it's only for a little while, remember?" The lump in his throat grew and swelled to an unbearable agony. "I promised you, didn't I? Just . . . for a little while, love."

He felt the dampness of her tears mingling with his own, and he pulled in a ragged but determined breath. "Charles is waiting for you, love. Go now. I can't bear this any longer."

With great tenderness, he reached to loosen her hold around his neck and pushed her gently away from him.

Kerry gave him one last devastating look of anguish. Then, blinded with her own tears, she turned and ran to where Charles was waiting to help her board the train.

Jess stood, his hand upraised in a feeble wave, his desolate, unhappy gaze following the train as it gradually disappeared from view. Unexpectedly, the sight of the train moving off into the distance caused his thoughts to drift back to another day when Kerry had left him.

On that occasion, she had run away after convincing herself that she was no more to him than a troublesome thorn in his side. Half-crazed with fear and broken by her desertion, Jess found her in New York. There, they admitted their true feelings for each other and returned to West Point to be married.

But this was different; this time, he was sending her away. For a moment, he swayed on his feet. A faint roaring sound circled his head, and he suddenly felt extremely ill. His heartbeat fell apart, racing, then slowing with a jerk.

He shuddered and hugged his shoulders against an inexplicable chill spreading down the length of his spine. For one dark, agaonizing moment, he saw Kerry's face—pale with fear, frozen in a silent scream of terror. The blood-freezing image disappeared as quickly as it had come, leaving him badly shaken and weak to the point of numbness.

He made his way to a bench and collapsed on it, drawing several curious glances from people rushing by. He didn't know how long he sat there, frightened, dazed, and desperately searching his mind to understand what had just happened to him. Finally, he leaned back wearily and closed his eyes. He wished with all his heart that he had gone with her, knowing he wouldn't draw an easy breath until Charles returned with word that she was safely ensconced at the home of his aunt. Already he was doubting the wisdom of what he'd done; already he was feeling the inconsolable desolation of her absence.

CHAPTER FIFTEEN

The city was as crowded, noisy, and intimidating as Kerry remembered it. She felt dwarfed by the milling crowds pressing around them as Charles tried to find a hack. She had always found New York to be depressing; she thought it particularly so today.

The cobbled streets glistened with a cold rain that was no more than a degree or two away from being sleet. It was not yet evening, but the afternoon was gray and dismal. She shivered in her fur-trimmed cloak as the harsh wind pelted her face with stinging rain.

A dandy in an elegant coat and silk hat poked her rudely with his walking stick as he strolled by, only seconds before a vendor, hurrying along through the mob, stepped on her foot with enough force to make her cry out. The entire area was a teeming mass of laughter and bickering, peddlers and businessmen, velvet and canvas, the clatter of wagons, the shouting of children, and the language of uncounted nations. All was confusion and clamor, and Kerry, exhausted by an aching heart and a throbbing head, wanted nothing more than to get away and find some quiet.

133

She felt an enormous sense of relief when Charles led her to an enclosed carriage a few feet away and helped her inside. His instructions to the driver, however, puzzled her.

"Charles, are you sure that's the right address?" she questioned as he climbed into the carriage beside her. "That doesn't sound like the street name Jess wrote down for us."

Briskly rubbing his hands together to warm them, the boyishly slender young man frowned at Kerry blankly. "The right address?" His thin, deeply hollowed face then relaxed with understanding. "Oh, I'm sorry, Mrs. Dalton, I forgot to tell you. The pastor asked me to pick up some books and things for him before I return to Washington. I thought I'd just make a quick stop on the way if you don't mind."

Kerry did mind, not wanting to stop anywhere until she reached a warm house and a bit of peace and quiet. But she only nodded a silent assent and turned her attention to the scene outside the carriage as they began to move.

America . . . where the streets are paved with gold, she thought cynically, glancing out at the crowded, littered streets. The splendor of richly dressed pedestrians going merrily along their way was rudely marred by starving children, old men bowed by the indignity of begging, and young women dragging themselves along, looking half-alive, and trying to protect their small babies from the cold.

As the carriage clattered along for what seemed to be an interminable length of time, Kerry continued to stare dejectedly outside. At least fifteen or twenty minutes passed before she realized that their surroundings were undergoing a drastic change. The neighborhoods behind them appeared to be a combination of business districts and lower-class residential areas. Though gloomy and crowded, they had nevertheless looked respectable enough.

Now, peering out for a closer look, Kerry saw that a marked transformation had occurred. Without a doubt, they were in the midst of a slum area, and an incredibly deplorable one at that.

The street, rather than being cobbled, was no more than a rut of mud framed by dingy tenement houses, all alike and closely crammed together. Story after story rose above the ground, shutting out almost all that was left of the late afternoon light. Pigs

134

ran loose in the streets, dilapitated breweries and dismal factory buildings hovered above ramshackle dwellings, and on every corner young toughs lunged indolently or shoved one another about. All the buildings were dingy red brick or rotting, unpainted frame. Kerry had an instant sense of squalor and congestion, and she caught a strong, unpleasant whiff of brewery odors mixed with rotting food and horse droppings.

She darted a quizzical look at Charles. The quiet young secretary appeared more tense than usual, but he seemed to be unaware of Kerry's growing dismay.

"Charles, are you certain you know where we're going?" she asked, her tone edged with doubt.

He looked at her and blinked. "Why . . . yes. Of course, Mrs. Dalton."

"Then perhaps we should learn whether our driver knows what he's about," Kerry snapped, her nerves frayed from fatigue and anxiety.

"Oh, I'm sure he does," Charles said soothingly.

Kerry, however, didn't miss the odd, somewhat anxious glint in his eyes. She looked out once more, then turned back to Charles, touching his forearm lightly. "Please, Charles—I think you should inquire. I can't imagine that this is the sort of neighborhood where you'd find what Jess ordered."

Charles appeared to consider her suggestion for a moment but did nothing. Nor did he offer a comment. Kerry studied him with growing bewilderment and vexation as he continued to stare straight ahead.

She felt her stomach begin to tighten and rebel at the thickening assault of offensive smells and her own growing alarm. This time when she spoke, her voice was sharp and far more authoritative.

"Charles—I want you to stop this carriage right now, please!"

He turned and stared at her, and Kerry swallowed hard at the look in his eyes. It suddenly occurred to her with a sickening sense of dread that something was terribly wrong here.

Jess's secretary was ordinarily a quiet, retiring young man who went about his affairs with downcast eyes and very little display of emotion. But the hostile glare he now turned on her glistened with an unfamiliar slyness she had never seen before.

Kerry spoke his name once more, in a tight, apprehensive tone. "Charles?"

He ignored her. Kerry felt a chilling wave of panic seize her as she watched his chiseled, expressionless face. Her mind whirled, and for an instant she found herself unable to think or move. Somehow, she willed herself to swallow her fear and act. Moving swiftly to lean against the door of the carriage, she hung her head out and shouted as loudly as she could. "Driver! Stop this carriage at once!"

Charles, stunned by her action, recovered quickly enough to snake his arm out and pull her roughly back inside, interposing his body over hers. Thrusting his head out, he shouted his own instructions to the driver. "The lady is ill, driver—just continue as you were. Take us to the address I gave you—as speedily as possible!"

Pulling himself back inside, he retained his grasp on her arm. "Please don't try that again, Mrs. Dalton. It'll be best if you simply cooperate."

"Cooperate!" Kerry stared at him with stunned disbelief. "Are you daft, Charles? What is this all about? Where do you think you're taking me?"

Instead of answering, he clamped his jaw rigidly shut and, still holding her arm in a painfully tight grip, he glanced from one side of the carriage to the other with wild, feverishly bright eyes. The driver, however, had heard Kerry call out and slowed the horses. Charles flicked his gaze to her face.

"Mrs. Dalton, tell the driver to go on," he rasped furiously.

"Indeed, I won't " Kerry retorted. She lifted her chin defiantly, her eyes blazing with anger. "And I'll thank you to let go of my arm at once, Charles Payne! I can't imagine what you're thinking of, but I can tell you that you're in trouble unless you—"

"Be quiet!" he hissed.

Seeing the enraged glint in his eyes, Kerry sensed, for the first time, how enormously disturbed the young man actually was. She felt a definite stab of fear as she looked away from him.

The carriage came to a complete stop, and Payne's face turned crimson. "Driver, come here, please! At once!" he called out.

Kerry held her breath, trying desperately to think what to do. When the driver approached the window of the carriage on Charles's side, she leaned forward with the intention of crying out. But Payne pushed her roughly back against the seat, still maintaining a relentless grip on her forearm as he turned to the driver.

"I'm afraid—the lady is quite beside herself," he said with attempted smoothness. "She's had a terrible shock, you see, and it's caused her a great emotional disturbance."

The driver peered inside the carriage, his lined, weathered face suspicious and questioning.

"Please, driver, help me!" Kerry cried, her words spilling out in a rush.

"Say, what's going on here—"

Suddenly, Charles pulled a gun from inside his coat and shoved it close to the driver's face. "Now you listen to me—" he shouted in a high, shrill voice while the hand holding the gun trembled violently. "You get back up where you belong and take us to the address I gave you, or—"

Momentarily stunned by the sight of the pistol in Charles's hand, Kerry acted on instinct, sensing this might be her only chance to escape.

While Payne's attention was still diverted from her to the driver, she yanked herself free of his grasp, pushed the door open, and jumped from the carriage, taking off in a run.

Startled, Charles yelled after her, lunged from the carriage, and began to chase her. Kerry glanced back. When she saw him behind her, she increased her speed as much as possible on the slick, mud-pitted street. She ran like a wild animal, her heart pounding furiously as she darted between ragged children and tough, angry-looking men.

At the entrance to a narrow alley, she stopped to look desperately around for a way to lose Charles, who was rapidly gaining on her. Making a split-second decision, she turned into the alley, clutching her purse against her chest with both hands as if to stop the pounding of her heart. She ran down the narrow alley and darted into a cobbled street lined with ramshackle tenements.

When she looked back and saw that Charles was no longer

behind her, she nearly cried with relief. She slowed her pace for an instant and tried to catch her breath; she knew she had to keep running to put as much distance as possible between her and Payne. But the street was slick, and she slipped. Twisting her foot she fell sharply on one side of her ankle. The unexpected pain threw her completely off balance, and both feet went out from under her, causing her to fall face forward in the street.

By now Kerry was irrational with panic. She scrambled to her knees, forcing herself by sheer strength of will to ignore her scraped chin and hands. Hauling herself to her feet, she once more began to run, all the while looking wildly around in search of a place to hide. Hot tears streamed down her cheeks as she half ran, half stumbled through the street. The pain in her ankle made her feel faint and nauseous, and she was terrified she might pass out, knowing it would be the end of her if she did.

Suddenly she stopped, her eyes focusing on a drab tenement house directly across from her. The door was ajar, and a small boy stood in the doorway, staring curiously out at her.

Kerry locked her gaze with his for an instant, then glanced frantically back at the way she'd come. She had lost Charles, at least for the moment. But she had also lost her purse—most likely when she fell—and with it, the paper on which Jess had written his Aunt Marian's address. Now she had no idea where to go, even if she could remain free long enough to get there.

She dared not go back to look for the purse; Charles might turn into the alley any instant.

As she stood there, frantically trying to figure out what to do, the sound of a small, steady voice cut into her thoughts. "Is something wrong, missus?"

It was the little boy in the doorway. Kerry stared at him thoughtfully for a moment, then impulsively hurried over to him.

He studied her for a time before offering to move aside from the partially opened door so she could enter.

He was a peculiar little mite, Kerry thought as she stared down at him. He looked to be no more than six or seven years old, thin as a twig, but seemingly healthy. A thick mop of curls the color of a new copper coin topped his head like a jaunty cap, framing a narrow, somewhat delicate face. Eyes as green as a shamrock hill and sober with the wisdom of old sorrows carefully measured her. His muslin shirt was little more than a rag, his baggy trousers patched to the maximum. Yet, Kerry sensed she was being weighed by a formidable intelligence and a spirit of great depth.

"There's a man—" she gasped, barely able to get the words out. "He mustn't catch me! Will you hide me, lad?"

He blinked. "Is he a badman, then?"

Kerry nodded desperately. "Please—can you hide me?"

He considered her plea for only an instant, then nodded and closed the door. "Aye, you can come up to our place. Me Mum went to pick up the piecework, and I was watching for her. I'll take you to our room, then come back."

He led the way up a narrow, rickety staircase. Pausing at the landing of the third floor, he gestured for Kerry to follow him. At the end of a dark hall reeking of sour food odors and decay, he stopped, pushed open a badly-warped door, and waited for Kerry to go inside.

"This is our room," he told her, following her over the threshold. "Me mum says it's one of the best to have. Only the rooms in front and back have windows, you see," he explained with a slight note of pride in his voice.

He stood only inches away from her, as if he were waiting for something. Finally, he reached out his hands, and Kerry realized with surprise that he was offering to take her wrap.

"You can stay here while I go back downstairs and watch for Mum," he said as he hung her wet cloak on a wall hook. "'Tis not a neighborhood for a woman to walk alone in, don't you see, so I wait for her each day."

Panting heavily from her frantic race through the streets and the hasty ascent of the stairs, Kerry nodded with relief. "What's your name, lad?" He's such a peculiar, serious little thing, she thought.

"Casey Fitzgerald, missus. Mum calls me Casey-Fitz."

"An old name, and one to be proud of," remarked Kerry automatically. "How long since you came?"

"Almost two months now."

"Your whole family?"

"There's only me and Mum. Maureen Fitzgerald is her name."

He paused a moment, then added, "Da started with us but he died on the way."

"I'm sad for you, Casey-Fitz. I, too, lost someone I loved aboard a ship a few years ago. My only brother."

He nodded as if he had heard the story many times before. "There's a bit of a fire there in the cook stove, if you're cold," he told her, motioning to a small ancient stove in the corner of the room.

Kerry glanced about her surroundings with concealed dismay. The entire room wasn't as large as the smallest bedroom in the parsonage, and yet it was obviously the total living quarters for the boy and his mother. A rickety cot sat in front of the room's only window and apparently served as both bed and couch. In the middle of the room stood a rough-hewn table with two chairs, one of them with a broken back. A number of pieces of material and clothing were strewn across the table. A tattered upholstered chair cowered against one wall. Beside it sat a small oil lamp on a spindly-legged table. The room was airless, dreary, and quite cold, but as clean and tidy as possible, given its furnishings.

Kerry turned back to the boy. "I'm extremely grateful to you, Casey-Fitz, for letting me come here. Oh, my name is Kerry, by the way—Mrs. Kerry Dalton."

"It's fine to be meeting you, I'm sure, Mrs. Dalton."

Kerry smiled at his attempt to be mannerly under the bizarre circumstances. "You may call me Kerry, if you like. Incidentally, Casey-Fitz, I'm from Ireland, too."

He nodded as if he had known it all along. He smiled then for the first time, only a hint of a softening around his mouth, but Kerry thought again that he had quite a remarkable face. It was a face that spoke of an ancient Celtic nobility, subtly touched with an earthiness and a sharp intellect far more developed than usually seen in one so young.

"I must go now," he said abruptly before turning to hurry from the room. "I'll be back soon with Mum."

After the lad left, Kerry studied the room once more, then walked over to look out the window. There was nothing to see except a dreary brick wall a few feet away. As she stood staring woodenly outside, the hopelessness of her situation engulfed her.

Charles Payne, a man both she and Jess had trusted for months, had, for some inconceivable reason, attempted to abduct her. Had she not escaped when she did, he might even have harmed her, the way he waved that pistol around. Where had he intended to take her—and why?

Common sense told her that he was, in some way at least, implicated in the terrible nightmare of incidents that had been happening ever since their move to Washington. But she couldn't being to fathom the connection.

Now, here she was, in this cold, dismal room, at the mercy of strangers who obviously had no means of helping her. She hadn't a prayer of finding her way to Jess's Aunt Marian without the address, which was written on a piece of paper in her lost purse. Nor had she any money to pay for assistance. Her valise was still in the carriage; she had only the clothes on her back. She didn't know where she was or how to get away.

Merciful Father, how do I get out of this? She tried desperately to push down the coil of despair springing up inside her. She must keep her wits about her. Perhaps the boy and his mother could help, although she couldn't imagine how, seeing the dire straits they seemed to be in themselves.

Hearing footsteps on the stairs, she turned uneasily toward the door, holding her breath and wondering what kind of reception she might encounter from Maureen Fitzgerald.

CHAPTER SIXTEEN

The door opened on a small, frail-looking woman with frightened eyes. Casey-Fitz followed her inside, carrying a large basket heaped with pieces of material. The woman looked at Kerry for only a moment before turning to shut the door after her son.

With a tired sigh, she walked over to the table and cleared a place for Casey to set the basket, then raised her eyes to stare at Kerry with an anxious frown.

She wore a faded cotton dress and a ragged shawl, and her light brown hair was pulled into a careless knot at the nape of her neck. Her clothing was nearly threadbare, and she was far too thin. In spite of this, a quiet, understated loveliness and a hint of inner strength emanated from her.

Casey-Fitz took his mother by the hand and presented her as grandly as if she were a queen. "This is me mum, Maureen Fitzgerald. Mrs. Kerry Dalton is the lady's name, Mum."

The woman's gaze flickered from Kerry's face to the obviously expensive cloak hanging on the wall hook. "The boy says you're in trouble." Her voice was unexpectedly soft, but Kerry heard the definite note of apprehension in it.

She nodded quickly. "Your son was good enough to help me, Mrs. Fitzgerald. He's a fine lad."

Maureen Fitzgerald nodded as she pulled her shawl more tightly around her. "We can't have trouble here, Mrs. Dalton. It's only the boy and me, and I've nowhere else to be going. What is it you want from us, then?"

"Oh, I want nothing, Mrs. Fitzgerald!" Kerry assured her. "There's a man, you see, who tried to—take me somewhere I didn't want to go. I had to get away from him and find my husband's aunt, for that's where my Jess thinks I am—" Kerry stopped in midsentence, realizing she was making no sense.

She drew in a steadying breath and attempted once more to explain slowly and clearly to Maureen Fitzgerald the events that had brought her to the flat. Maureen interrupted her only once, to indicate that she was to sit down at the table. "I have a bit of tea. I'll make us some while you talk."

Kerry sank gratefully onto the hard wooden chair and continued her explanation, stopping only long enough to take a deep sip of the tea Maureen brought back from the stove.

"So you see, Mrs. Fitzgerald, I somehow have to find Jess's aunt so I can get word to my husband. He has no idea where I am or what's happened. I can't imagine what Charles Payne was about, but I'm terrified that all this is part of a scheme to do harm to Jess. I must make my way to his Aunt Marian's somehow—but I can't remember even a part of her address, except that the street had a number twenty in it."

The boy had come to stand beside his mother's chair as he listened. He said nothing while Kerry told her story, but simply stood quietly with a protective hand on his mother's thin shoulder. The small, unhealthy-looking woman nodded when Kerry finished. "Sure and you've had a time of it, Mrs. Dalton." Her large, sober gray eyes searched Kerry's face for a long moment before she turned to look at her son.

It was Casey-Fitz who assumed the decision. "Couldn't we help Kerry, Mum?" he asked seriously.

"Mrs. Dalton, son," his mother corrected.

"She said I could call her Kerry."

144

"Did she now?" She gave him a soft smile. "Well, then, and I suppose you can. Do you have an idea how we can help, Casey-Fitz?"

"Not yet," he said matter-of-factly. "But perhaps by morning I'll think of a way."

Maureen looked at the boy as if she had no doubt at all he would do just that. When she turned back to Kerry, her tired eyes held a steady light of warmth. "You're welcome to stay the night with us—or longer, if need be, Mrs. Dalton. But I fear I have no other means of helping you."

"To stay is enough—Maureen. I'm more than grateful just for that." Kerry reached across the table to touch the young woman, disturbed by the frail, delicate texture of her slender hand.

"I'll fix us a bite to eat." Maureen rose wearily from her chair. "Then I must be at my piecework."

Kerry quickly stood up. "Please—don't fix anything for me, Maureen," she insisted, uncertain as to whether these two would have enough food for another mouth. Besides, she was far too upset to even think of eating. "I'm afraid I couldn't bear the taste of food right now."

The boy surprised her by coming around to her side and taking her hand. With a sober look of understanding, he said, "It's all right. We have enough."

She looked down at his small, dreamy-serious face for a moment, then tousled his curly hair affectionately. "Thank you, lad. But I'm afraid I simply couldn't eat right now."

He nodded acceptingly and went to help his mother. "You go ahead and start your work, Mum. I'll warm the soup."

"Is this your work, then, Maureen?" Kerry asked, gesturing to the stacks of piecework on the table.

"Aye, it is for now. I go each morning to stand at the factory gate while they call the names. Eventually, I hope to get on inside. But for now, I do the piecework to keep us from going hungry."

"I'll help you tonight, then," Kerry told her, wanting to do something for this sad little woman who was being so kind to her. "Sure, and I need something to keep my hands busy."

At first Maureen looked doubtful, but then her gaze cleared as if she understood. "If you're certain you'd want to do that, Mrs.—

145

Kerry—I'd be more than glad for the help."

They worked long hours into the night, sewing trousers and trims, with Casey-Fitz helping them. The two women talked as they worked, trading stories of their homeland and families. Kerry told Maureen about her own coming over, about her da and Jess. She spoke longingly of their days at West Point, their courtship, and his ministry in Washington. She even revealed the terrible things that had happened to them, with the exception of losing the baby.

Maureen in turn confided that her husband had been given a bit of money by his grandfather, whose farm had been prosperous before the potato crop failed. They used the small gift of money to pay their fare to America. Unfortunately, Casey's father sickened on the way and died on board the "coffin ship," leaving his wife and son alone and their money severely depleted by the time they reached New York.

"Thank the good Lord I had enough left to pay for this room for us," Maureen said quietly, looking up from her piecework. "That plus the work I've been able to get has allowed us to live by ourselves here, rather than being cramped into a room with several others. Many in this building are living three or more families to a room, you see. I don't want that for Casey-Fitz, but I don't know how long I'll be able to avoid it, unless I get on at the factory."

Kerry's heart ached for them. They seemed so brave and fine, she thought, to be in such a desperate situation.

If I get out of this mess I'm in and back to Jess, somehow I'll repay the Fitzgeralds for their kindness.

After a few hours, Kerry saw Maureen's head begin to nod and her shoulders sag even as she continued to work. Casey, who had worked indefatigably alongside the women, immediately got up and went to his mother. Quietly and gently, he removed the material from her hands and laid it on the table. Then he tugged her to her feet, very carefully draping her arm over his small shoulder.

"Come on, now, Mum," he said softly, much as an adult would croon to a child. "You must be getting some rest."

He half-dragged his small mother over to the bed, eased her onto it, then very gently pulled a thin, shabby quilt over her still form.

Returning to the table, he resumed the work.

146

"Casey-Fitz," Kerry said softly, "don't you think you ought to get a bit of rest as well?"

His gaze met hers across the table. "I don't need as much sleep as Mum, you see. She's not a bit well. I'll just finish her quota first."

Kerry's throat tightened, and she quickly lowered her head so the boy woudn't see the pity she was feeling. "It's a fine thing, Casey-Fitz, for a woman to have a noble son like yourself. You must be a great joy to your mother."

"Don't you have any children, then, Kerry? He looked at her with compassion.

"I'm afraid not," she said quietly, unable to stop the thought of the tiny son she had never seen. Deliberately changing the subject, she looked up and him and asked, "Do you think about what you'd like to do when you're grown, Casey-Fitz? Have you a special dream for yourself?"

He glanced at her shyly, then looked away. "Aye, there are some things I'd like to do," he said solemnly. "First, I'd like to go home—back to Ireland. There are things there I want to see again, and some things I want to learn. Then I want to come back to America and help our people here. I'm going to be a doctor, you see."

"Ah, a doctor! That's lovely!" Kerry smiled across at him. "And what is it you want to learn about Ireland?"

He considered her question, coloring slightly. "You won't be laughing at me, if I tell you?"

"Of course I won't laugh at you, Casey-Fitz," Kerry assured him gravely.

He nodded accepting her word. "I want to learn all the old stories and songs, and then bring them back here to keep for our people."

Kerry stared at him. What manner of child-man was this? "Their hero legends and the tales of the Faery, you mean?"

He nodded his head enthusiastically. "Those, and the old songs." Something else seemed to occur to him then, and he added, "I think I'd like to be a harper, as well."

"That would be a fine thing, too. You like music, then?"

His smile was dreamy and distant, and his eyes took on a glow even as his hands continued to work the material. "More than anything. Da, he had such a voice. Mum said he could charm the birds from the bushes."

"I know a fine harper," Kerry told him, smiling at the memory of Mackenzie. "I should like you to meet him one day. He's a grand friend, and he plays the clairseach* and the squeeze-box, and all sorts of instruments. He, too, had a big, fine voice."

"You told Mum that your husband is a preacher-man."

"Aye, he is," Kerry said softly, "and a wonderful man he is, Casey-Fitz." Her eyes glistened with pride and love. "Jess Dalton is a giant of a man, in stature and in heart, as much as any warrior of the Fianna* ever was," she said fondly.

Casey grinned at her. "Your face sparkles when you talk about him."

Surprised, Kerry laughed at herself. "Well, so does my heart, Casey-Fitz, and that's the truth of it."

For the next hour, she entertained the boy as they worked, telling him stories from her own collection of the old legends, adding to what he already knew of Cuchulain, Lugh of the Long Arm, Deirdre, and Queen Maeve. She recited a number of the exploits of Finn MacCuhal, the great leader of the Fianna*, who was said to have eaten of the Salmon of Knowledge to gain all the wisdom of the world.

"And I think it's a wise thing for a lad like yourself to remember, Casey-Fitz, that no man—even a brave champion like Finn Mac-Cuhal—could join the strong warriors of the Fianna* unless they knew the old legends and poetry and could recite from them. Even the most famous warriors among the ancient ones, you see, were judged on more than their strength and bravery."

So fascinated he'd nearly forgotten his work, Casey asked with bright-eyed interest, "The Fianna* were poets, too?"

"Oh, indeed they were—and isn't that the way of a true Irish hero, though? Part poet, part warrior, and part singer."

After two or three more stories, Kerry taught him the song "Drimeen" and some other old ballads. They sang softly together so they wouldn't wake Maureen. The long night made them friends, and their love for the land they had left—its legends, its music, and its magic—brought the two of them together in a way time itself never could have.

CHAPTER SEVENTEEN

The next morning, Jess paced impatiently back and forth in Senator Forbrush's waiting room, frequently glancing from the office door to the secretary's vacant desk.

His curiosity had been growing ever since the afternoon before, when Lowell Martin, Forbrush's aide, had brought a message from the senator requesting that Jess meet with him in his senate office at nine o'clock this morning.

At the moment, however, he was more apprehensive about Kerry than anything else. He couldn't understand why Charles wasn't back by now. He'd been certain the secretary would show up at the church office early this morning to report on the trip to New York. When he hadn't arrived by the time Jess had to leave for his meeting with Forbrush, he seriously considered canceling the appointment. Only the possibility that it was something of real importance spurred him to go.

While Preston Forbrush had never been openly hostile to him, for weeks he had made it clear that he opposed every principle to which Jess had dedicated his life. For his part, Jess knew little about the famous senator other than what the Washington rumor mill had provided him: Forbrush was an awesomely wealthy man. It was thought that he had accumulated much of his wealth by questionable means. There were occasional whisperings of Forbrush's involvement in a number of practices Jess detested as immoral, even illegal.

Some of his more lurid dealings were said to include slave trading, prostitution, and vote buying. His facility for getting away with all of it was obvious since he was one of the most powerful and feared politicians in Washington.

Jess wasn't naive enough to think Forbrush had experienced a sudden change of heart about him. He was hoping, however, that perhaps the senator had at least decided to cease his recent defamation campaign against Jess and his ministry. He wondered, too, if this morning's meeting had anything to do with the upcoming Senate address.

The senator's office door opened suddenly; startled, Jess jumped and turned around.

"Ah, good morning, Pastor," Forbrush said cheerfully, making a sweeping motion with his arm to indicate that Jess should enter. "I'm pleased you were able to meet with me on such short notice."

The diminutive gray-haired senator appeared even smaller when he stepped back to allow Jess entrance to his office. Forbrush was often underestimated, Jess had heard, because of his small, almost delicate physical appearance; Jess suspected that it was a mistake one seldom made more than once.

Glancing around the massive, lavishly furnished office with its enormous monument of a desk, Jess was surprised to see Lowell Martin. The younger man nodded his head curtly and remained standing in front of the long, velvet-draped window.

"Please, sit down, Pastor," Forbrush offered, lowering himself gracefully into the large leather chair behind his desk.

The senator, Jess thought ruefully, had a way of making a man feel awkward and somewhat ponderous, no matter how correctly he might be dressed. His own sensible black suit suddenly seemed poorly tailored and out of style on his large frame. He sat down in a comfortable leather chair opposite Forbrush. The much smaller man on the other side of the desk appeared fastidiously neat and impeccably groomed, his dark suit obviously expensive and custom-designed.

Jess felt a prickling of irritation when he realized Forbrush apparently intended to take his time in revealing the purpose of the meeting. Indeed, he ruefully admitted to himself, there was little that wouldn't irritate him this morning.

He hadn't slept at all during the night, his mind plaguing him with the memory of those last few moments with Kerry at the train station—the way she had clung to him, her tear-filled eyes begging him to change his mind. The sight of her petite, forlorn figure as she started toward the train, the way she had continued to glance back at him until she disappeared inside the passenger car, had haunted him hour after endless hour. The last thing he felt like doing right now was playing cat-and-mouse with Preston Forbrush.

A glance at Martin set him even more on edge. For some reason, the coldly handsome young man was virtually smirking at Jess, his light hazel eyes raking him with what could only be amused contempt. Unsettled, Jess transferred his gaze back to the senator. A disturbing needle of foreboding made the hair at the back of his neck tingle when he found Forbrush staring at him with the same expression of humorous scorn.

Finally, the senator broke the silence. "Well, Pastor, no doubt you're wondering why I asked you to come here this morning." His southern drawl was smooth and casual.

Jess inclined his head slightly, waiting.

"Of course you are," Forbrush said, his smile broadening. "Well, sir, the fact of the matter is that we have a proposition for you." He stared at Jess expectantly.

"What kind of proposition would that be, Senator?" With some effort, Jess kept his tone bland but courteous.

Forbrush rested his elbows on the desktop and laced his fingers together. "We have something . . . to trade . . . in return for your cooperation, Mr. Dalton."

Out of the corner of his eye, Jess saw Martin's sneer deepen. He remained silent, waiting for Forbrush to go on.

"Ah—of course. You're probably wondering what in the world I'm talking about, aren't you?" He hesitated, his smile fixed in place. "I've decided, Pastor, that it would really be in everyone's best interests—including your own—for you to resign your pulpit and leave Washington. Right away."

A strong wave of disappointment and surprise washed over Jess. Certainly he hadn't expected anything like this. "I think you know I won't do that, Senator," he said quietly.

"Well, now, that would have been true, I'm sure, until recently, you being the determined young man that you are," Forbrush remarked agreeably. "However, you're also known to be an intelligent, reasonable man as well, Pastor, so I'm positive you'll have a change of heart once you hear my proposition."

"I rather doubt that, Senator." Jess deliberately kept his voice even and steady, but his mind was racing. What was Forbrush up to?

"Oh, I wouldn't be too hasty to dismiss the possibility, if I were you, Mr. Dalton. At least, not until you've heard me out."

Jess made a small motion with his head to indicate his willingness to listen.

"Lowell, why don't you explain to the pastor why it's so important to us that he leave Washington?" Forbrush suggested slyly to his aide.

Martin took a step forward from his stance in front of the window. "Of course, Senator."

Jess wasn't a man easily intimidated, but he felt a definite stab of apprehension when he saw the undisguised hatred and contempt in Martin's gaze.

"What Senator Forbrush would like you to understand, Mr. Dalton," the aide said in a tone that dripped sarcasm, "is that you're simply not welcome in Washington any longer. Not," he added pointedly, "that you ever were. You're causing a great deal of undesirable confusion about issues that are really none of your business. You see, sir, to be brutally frank, you're a fool. Even worse, you're a dangerous fool. That's why you really must take your leave."

Jess started to his feet, but immediately forced down the rage boiling up in his throat at Martin's insult. He swallowed with difficulty and gripped the arms of his chair, but said nothing.

Forbrush studied Jess's face carefully before he spoke. "Forgive my aide's somewhat rash words, Pastor. The young do

152

tend to be . . . indelicate at times, I'm afraid. Still, I must agree with Martin; you're simply not welcome in Washington."

"If you're finished, Senator," Jess said heavily, again starting to rise from his chair, "I have other things to do."

"But I'm not finished," Forbrush snapped. "I offered you a proposition. Don't you even want to hear the rest of it?"

"There's absolutely nothing you could say to me that I'd be interested in hearing, Senator," Jess said with distaste, turning to leave the office.

"I wouldn't be too sure of that," Forbrush objected quickly. "Unless, of course, you no longer have any affection for that pretty little Irish wife of yours."

Jess whirled around, feeling his face burn with sudden anger and alarm. "What are you talking about?"

"Calm yourself, Pastor. It isn't seemly for a man of the cloth to show his temper, you know." Forbrush was obviously intent upon humiliating Jess.

"What about my wife?" Jess rasped. He moved swiftly to Forbrush's desk, bracing both hands on its smooth top as he leaned threateningly toward the mocking senator.

Forbrush blinked, wincing slightly. "Simply this," he answered after a slight hesitation. Meeting Jess's angry stare with an impassive glance, he stated flatly, "Your wife is now being held by some people who work for me in New York City. She is quite unharmed and will remain so if you cooperate. If you don't . . ." He let his words fall away meaningfully.

"That's a lie!" Jess shouted, knotting his hand into a sturdy fist and slamming the desk with a loud thud.

Forbrush stood abruptly; if he felt cowed by the immense, furious man across the desk from him, he concealed it well. His voice was even, his gaze level as he replied, "No, Pastor, it is not a lie. I realize that you have been, until this moment, unaware of the situation. But the fact of the matter is that your wife is not at the home of your aunt, as you believe. She had been taken captive and is in a location known only to me and a few select men who work for me."

Jess felt his hands and legs begin to tremble. Kerry—they had Kerry? No! That was impossible. He'd seen her leave with Charles on the train, had seen the train leave the station on its way to New York. Charles was escorting her to his Aunt Marian's. Charles wouldn't let . . . "Charles?"

He was unaware that he'd said his secretary's name aloud until Forbush answered with a cold smile. "Ah, yes. Another disappointment for you, I'm sure, Dalton. But you see, Charles does only what he's told to do. It's nothing personal, you understand."

His heart suddenly went crazy, his mind reeling with fear. They had to be lying. Surely they were trying to bluff him. They couldn't possibly have Kerry . . . unless it were true, about Charles . . .

Martin crossed his arms over his chest and gave a low, ugly laugh. The look of absolute cruelty on his face froze Jess's blood.

"Try not to worry, Mr. Dalton. The boys will take good care of your wife. Oh, it's true that they may be a bit crude sometimes, but they're not bad fellows. They may have a little fun with her, but they won't hurt her, I'm sure."

The sound that erupted from Jess could have been the roar of an enraged wild animal. He would have charged the younger man like an angry lion had the door to the office not exploded open on a wild-eyed, disheveled Charles Payne.

His attention diverted for the moment from Martin, Jess turned and lunged toward Payne. "Where is she?" he demanded furiously, catching the front of Charles's shirt in his hand. "Where did you take her?"

The secretary's face drained of all color as he stared up into Jess's burning eyes. "I . . . she . . ."

"Where?" Desperate beyond all endurance, Jess continued to clutch Payne by the shirt, blistering him with the heat of his anger.

"Let him go Dalton!"

Martin's voice cracked like a rifle shot. For an instant, Jess ignored him, continuing to stare down into Charles's unshaven, terrified face.

"I said—let him go, Dalton, or I'll blow your head off."

Jess looked back over his shoulder to see Martin holding a gun on him. Slowly, he turned back to Charles, then dropped his hand. But his gaze never left the younger man's face. "How could

154

you do this? Why?" His voice was rough with fear and ominously quiet.

Payne faltered, glancing from the gun in Martin's hand to the angry, wounded accusation in Jess's eyes. "They never told me I'd have to hurt anyone," he stammered, his look pleading for understanding.

Suddenly, he grabbed hold of Jess's arm. "It isn't as bad as you think. We never got there—to the place I was supposed to take her. She got away from me."

Forgetting the gun turned on him, Jess lowered his face so close to Payne's they almost touched. "What do you mean? Where is she?" he grated harshly.

"She ran away from me . . . in the streets. I wasn't . . . able to find her." He cowered when he saw Forbrush start toward him, a look of disbelief and rage on his face.

"Are you saying you never got her to the inn?" the senator asked with incredulous fury, moving in beside Jess to impale the trembling secretary with his piercing stare.

Without warning, Charles's expression began to crumble. He stared at Forbrush, then Martin, and finally Jess. Perspiration bathed his face as his entire body started to shake. "I couldn't help it," he muttered feebly. "I tried to stop her, but she ran. I searched for hours—I simply couldn't find her!"

Jess grabbed his arm. "But you remember where you were when she got away from you? You could take me there—"

Payne looked up at Jess with dazed eyes. "Take you? I—yes," he said distantly. Slowly, his gaze cleared.

"Yes—I'd remember, I think. Mr. Dalton, please believe me . . . I wouldn't have hurt her—I wouldn't!"

Jess glared down at the secretary with disgust. "It's been you all along? You and this bunch of madmen?" He made a wide, encompassing gesture with his arm. "Everything that's happened to us— to Kerry—you've been a part of it?" A mixture of disbelief and bewilderment crossed his face as he continued to search Payne's eyes.

"I—they never told me I'd have to hurt anyone. I didn't know it would lead to anything like this, I swear I didn't. They told me all I had to do was report your movements to them."

155

"But why, Charles?" Jess stared at him with undisguised hurt and disillusionment. "What ever possessed you to get involved with them in the first place? I've done nothing to you—you didn't even know me when I came here."

Charles hung his head in a silent gesture of shame.

"Go ahead, you sniveling little fool," Forbrush's icy voice broke the quiet. "Tell him why you were so quick to accept our offer." When Payne said nothing, the senator commanded again, "Tell him!"

Charles turned his ravaged eyes on Jess as if he were about to beg for mercy. Instead, Jess saw defeat and total resignation settle over his thin face. Unable to meet the pastor's gaze, Payne stared down at the floor as he began to speak in an oddly calm and toneless voice.

"My mother—is Julia Shelton."

Jess lifted his brows with surprise. Julia Shelton was the most popular, renowned hostess in Washington. For years she had reigned as society's darling, a queen bee of incredible influence and power. At present, she was about to marry the wealthy, influential southern senator, John Caylor Waldo.

"Julia Payne Shelton," Charles said pointedly, now raising his gaze from the floor to look directly at Jess. "Both my father and her second husband, George Shelton, are dead."

Jess stared at him, still unable to comprehend the significance of his words.

"The lady Shelton has quite a secret," supplied Lowell Martin from where he was standing a few feet away. He leveled a mocking stare at Charles. "You see, she is about to marry one of the biggest slave holders in the South—and certainly one of the most virulent anti-Northern politicians—and the poor man doesn't even know his intended is the granddaughter of a slave." He smiled, an ugly, contemptuous slash against his perfect features.

"They were going to give the story to the papers!" Payne cried. "They threatened to smear it all over Washington. I couldn't let them do that to her." He drew in a long, ragged breath, then continued. "Her entire life is wrapped up in this town. And she loves Senator Waldo, she truly does. They told me—if I'd cooperate with them—they'd keep her secret from becoming public. They even offered to set me up in a political career to make her proud of me." He glanced away from Jess's pitying gaze. "I've always been—a disappointment to my mother," he mumbled. "All I had to do was—"

"Betray me," Jess finished for him quietly, searching Charles's face.

Payne stared at him for a moment, then nodded. "Yes. I wouldn't have done it just for the career," he protested. "But I had to do it . . . for her."

"Oh, Charles," Jess murmured with great sadness. "We could have found another way if you had only told me. I would have helped you—"

"This is all quite touching," Forbrush interrupted with a scathing sneer of contempt. "But quite pointless, I'm afraid. The two of you know far too much. I fear we have no choice but to—ensure your silence."

He half-turned to his aide. "It would seem that Payne had some sort of mental collapse, wouldn't you say, Martin? Rushing in here like a madman, taking potshots at us, then shooting the famous abolitionist preacher and himself—" He clucked his tongue dramatically. "Such a shame, really."

With a curt nod of his head, he told Martin. "Do Payne first."

Martin darted an astonished glance at the senator. "Shoot him?" He hesitated, then added, "Your secretary—"

"Baker is in Virginia today, attending to some personal business for me. There is no one on the floor close enough to hear anything. Now do it!"

Martin still hesitated, looking from Payne to the senator. "There wasn't anything said about killing a man for you!"

"What did you expect, you simpleton?" Forbrush hissed. "That I'd sponsor you for nothing? Do as you're told!"

When Martin continued to waver, glancing nervously from Jess to Charles, Forbrush choked off an oath and grabbed the gun roughly out of his hand. "I should have known better than to take you on in the first place. Any offspring of a milksop like Thurman Martin couldn't have any backbone to him."

Forbrush angrily turned the gun on Charles and tightened his finger on the trigger.

Jess looked at the gun in Forbrush's hand, then at the expression in the senator's eyes. He knew he had no more than a second. Hunching one powerful shoulder, he shoved against Charles's side, pushing him out of the line of fire.

The force of Jess's move knocked Charles against the wall at the instant the gun exploded. Payne stared in horror as the big pastor took the bullet meant for him.

Jess weaved, staggered, and said only one word: "Kerry . . ."

As Charles watched Jess topple to the floor, he fumbled for his own gun. Managing to finally yank it from inside his coat, he slowly and deliberately aimed the pistol at Senator Preston Forbrush's heart.

Chapter Eighteen

A nagging feeling of dread settled over Kerry long before dawn, beginning with the eerie, blood-chilling howl that awakened her. A stray dog, she quickly told herself, one of the alley scavengers that traipsed about the city streets in search of food. But in those early, lonely hours before first light, she couldn't help but remember with a tingling of fear the stories of the banshee.

She'd grown up hearing about the warning wail in the night that foretold a death. But when her da had disavowed the old superstitions as contrary to their Christian faith, Kerry had followed his example. She knew deep inside herself that this wave of foreboding was most likely due to the terror of the day before and the frightening, precarious position in which she now found herself. Still, in the cold, dark hours before morning, she'd been able to discard the disturbing tales of the unearthly, shrieking harbinger of death only with concentrated prayer and determined force of will.

As the morning wore on, with Maureen gone to the factory and Casey-Fitz quietly working on cap trims, Kerry was again having uneasy feelings. Jess hadn't been out of her thoughts all morning. So strong was the pull of his dear smile and tender blue gaze that she had begun to wonder if something was wrong. Surely the bond between them was stronger than physical presence; she would know, wouldn't she, if things weren't right with him? And wouldn't he also know that things were not well with her?

She sighed, picked up a piece of material, and returned Casey's smile as she began to help him once more with the sewing. There was little she could do about the wild, implausible thoughts spinning through her mind. At least she would do what she could to keep her hands busy.

"You look happy this morning, Casey-Fitz," she observed, glancing at the boy working contentedly over a piece of material.

"True for you," he agreed. "I'm thinking Mum finally got on inside the factory. Otherwise, she'd have been back here long before now."

"That will make things better for the both of you, won't it?"

"Aye, Mum says it will. We're going to save every bit we can so we can have a proper house some day." A faint glimmer of hope lighted his eyes when he looked up at her.

"I'm glad for you, Casey-Fitz," Kerry said warmly. "Sure and the two of you deserve only good things."

He grinned at her, and Kerry thought he had quite the nicest smile she had ever seen, other than Jess's, of course.

"You like me mum a lot, don't you, Kerry?"

"Well, I certainly do. And I like her son every bit as much."

Her words made his smile grow even wider. "Kerry, is your husband really a giant?" A frown creased his high forehead as he studied her face.

She laughed and reached over to ruffle his hair. "He is that, Casey-Fitz, but not one from the legends. My Jess is a great man in stature, but his heart is even bigger, don't you see?" Her eyes misted for a moment and her smile turned bittersweet. "He has a heart so big he sometimes tries to hold the pain of the world in it," she said softly, looking down at her hands.

Recognizing her sadness, the boy made no reply but simply reached across the table to touch her hand uncertainly. Kerry glanced at him with surprise, then forced herself to answer his smile.

By midmorning, her back had begun to ache—as much, she suspected, from sleeping on a thin pallet on the floor as from hunching over the piecework hour after hour.

She got up, rubbed her shoulders distractedly, and walked to the window—not that there was anything to see except the same depressing brick wall. At least the ribbon of light visible between tenement buildings helped to banish the bleak drabness of the room.

What was Jess doing now, right this minute? she wondered with longing. Had Molly seen to it that he ate his breakfast? He was all too likely to go off without it if he was in a hurry. How would he manage to get his shirt-sleeves buttoned—he always fought them so—without her help? Was he missing her as sorely as she was missing him?

Casey-Fitz abruptly ended her troubled reverie, pushing in beside her at the window and tugging upward on its warped, swollen frame in an attempt to raise it.

"D'you hear, Kerry?" he cried excitedly, finally managing to lift the window a few inches. "It's the fire wagons!"

Kerry craned her neck, trying to see into the street below, but the buildings were too close together. She heard the distant fire bells, however, and the sound of frightened, confused cries.

"Let's go downstairs and watch the wagons!" Casey shouted, turning away from the window.

"Get your coat, lad," Kerry ordered, grabbing her cloak off the hook. "'Tis far too cold to stand outside without it."

By the time the two of them reached the downstairs doorway, horse-drawn fire wagons were racing through the street, followed by a mob of shouting people.

"'Tis the factory! The Bowden Factory's burning!" someone cried.

Kerry turned to look in the direction the fire wagons were headed and saw a dark gray spiral rising into the sky. A strong smell of smoke filled the air.

Casey started to run, then turned to grab Kerry's hand to pull her along with him. "The factory, Kerry! 'Tis the factory where Mum went!" he screamed. "Come on—we have to go to her!"

Panic struck her as she began to run with him through the

161

street. The sound of snorting, excited horses and clanging bells led the shouting crowd. The two of them were shoved and pushed aside more than once, but they forced their way back into the midst of the anxious mob and kept on running.

Kerry hadn't taken time to fasten her cloak, and now it fell from her shoulders. She left it in the street and continued to run. "Please, Lord, let her be all right!" she prayed desperately, ignoring the stitch in her side and forcing her legs to go even faster. Casey-Fitz kept a hold of her hand while his small feet flew over the cobbles. Eventually, they pulled away from the crowd and took the lead.

There was the sound of an explosion, then another, and behind them people began to scream and pray. Casey pointed up to the sky, not slowing his speed a fraction. "Look!"

Above the buildings Kerry saw thick black smoke, swirling debris, and shooting flames. They rounded a corner and stopped dead. The scene ahead of them was a hellish nightmare of exploding bricks and lapping flames. Firemen and police officers were trying to push back the crowd of stunned, panic-stricken people approaching the building, pressing closer and closer in an attempt to get to loved ones inside. Billowing smoke and flying embers were being picked up by the wind and whirled madly over the entire block.

The crowd behind them caught up with Kerry and Casey-Fitz; they were surrounded by loud keening and pleas for God's mercy. All was chaos, noise, and panic. Like a nightmare, sounds of pitiful screams came from inside the building. Kerry and the boy watched in silent horror as people began to jump to certain death. Many of them were already human torches when they plunged from the blazing inferno.

Still holding Casey's hand, Kerry started to move forward. The two of them were unable to take their terror-filled eyes off the burning brick building. Kerry heard a small voice beside her choke out one word—"Mum"—then he was gone.

Speechless, she watched the boy part the crowd and charge past spectators and through lines of firemen, their smoke-blackened faces wild with desperation as they worked furiously to halt the advance of the fire.

"Nooo . . . Casey . . . wait!"

Kerry panicked and froze for an instant, then began to run after him, crying his name as she raced into the crowd. She saw him slide by a burly fireman who tried in vain to block him; he then darted heedlessly into the burning building.

No longer conscious of what she was doing, Kerry plowed through the crowd, muttering mindlessly to herself as she forced her way to the gaping hole that had been the front entrance of the factory.

Merciful God, help me get him out of here, she prayed in desperation. A large hand reached out to stop her, and a hard block of a body tried to shove itself in front of her. But Kerry pushed on, choking on the dense, dark smoke, her eyes burning so fiercely she was almost blinded.

Inside the building, she screamed Casey's name and began looking aimlessly, wildly around to find him.

Suddenly she saw him, pinned behind a burning beam of wood, staring at her through enormous, terrified eyes. The smoke was worse, the heat was unbearable, and a path of flame snaked its way directly toward the boy. She stumbled forward across the floor, leaping over a mound of smoking rubble. Hoisting her skirt, she jumped the narrow lake of fire that threatened to engulf Casey-Fitz. Hurling herself at him, Kerry pushed him to safety only seconds before a blazing, falling timber would have crushed his small body beneath its deadly weight.

Staggering to keep her balance, she felt herself being quickly sucked into a spiraling tornado of smoke and flames. She heard a growing roar, a strange, whooshing sound above her, and finally a quiet hissing as something hit her head, then her shoulder. Stunned, she looked once at Casey before falling limply to the floor.

CHAPTER NINETEEN

I'm going to New York today, George," Jess emphatically stated to his doctor. "I feel fine—and I'm leaving today."

George Marshall sternly frowned at his patient. "You may feel perfectly fine, but you aren't—not yet. You've lost a great deal of blood, Jess, and you need at least another two or three days' rest before you do anything—much less get on a train."

Paying little attention to the harried doctor, Jess sat on the side of the bed, shirtless, hair tousled, his eyes shadowed. His left arm was contained in a sling; with his free hand, he rubbed his beard as though he were deep in thought.

When he finally spoke, it was with an edge of stubbornness that made the doctor realize he might as well save his breath. "I intend to be in New York by evening, George—" He lowered his voice but the determination in his gaze never faltered. "I have to find Kerry. It's been three days now since she . . . disappeared. Three days—and I've done nothing but lie here in bed . . . and bleed."

He stood up, wincing slightly from the effort, then quickly clamped his jaw into the firm, strong line all too familiar to the doctor. "On your way out," he told the doctor pointedly, "would you tell Mack I could use his help, please?" He motioned to his wounded arm and smiled ruefully. "I find I badly miss having two hands."

Dr. Marshall raked one hand through his light hair in a gesture of frustration. "Surely you don't intend to travel alone. You could pass out."

"I won't pass out, George," Jess hesitatingly replied with exaggerated patience. "How is Charles doing, by the way?"

Marshall twisted his mouth into a scowl of disapproval. "Better than he deserves. He'll be released from the hospital within the week. It's a lucky thing for him that Martin tried to shove the senator out of Payne's line of fire. Not only did his action save Forbrush's life, but it most certainly saved young Payne's as well. As it is, his rib cage may be extremely sore for a few days, but at least he's alive."

"Amazing," Jess said, going to the mirror to inspect his reflection, grimacing at what he saw. "At that close range, they could have easily killed each other."

Marshall nodded, watching Jess with clinical interest, as though he were waiting for some revealing sign of relapse.

"Well, Payne's bullet only winged the senator just as Martin knocked him to one side. And, of course, that shove was enough to throw off the senator's aim—so both of them got by with only superficial wounds. None of which might have been the case," added the doctor as he bent to open his medical bag, "if that senate guard hadn't heard all the ruckus and come by to check." Continuing to sort through the contents of his bag, he added, "Forbrush wasn't so badly hurt that he couldn't have killed both you and Payne had he not been stopped by the guard."

He walked over to Jess and said, "Sit down a moment and let me check that bandage." After satisfying himself that the wrapping on Jess's upper arm would do, he carefully replaced the sling.

When Jess again rose from the bed, Marshall studied him closely for a moment. "The police are going to be pressing you soon to sign those charges against Payne, you know," he said slowly. "Forbrush is all taken care of; he'll be locked up as soon as he recovers. And Martin and the rest of those thugs are in jail, of course. But Charles Payne's fate is still hanging."

"I know, I know," Jess said evasively. "I'll get to it later."

The doctor narrowed his eyes. "Pastor, you are going to press charges against that man, aren't you?" When Jess made no reply, he prodded. "Surely you wouldn't let him get away with what he did."

Jess shook his head and crossed the room to open the top drawer of the bureau. "No," he answered, fumbling for a shirt and pulling it out of the drawer. "He has to pay for what he did. But I'd like to talk to Kerry before signing anything. She's the one who has suffered most from all this, after all." He hesitated, then added softly, "But first I have to find her." He walked to the closet and began laying out clothing on the bed, one piece at a time.

"Pastor—Jess—would you please sit down for a moment? If you're determined to go today, there's something you need to know."

Jess turned around and glanced at Dr. Marshall with an impatient frown. "George, you're not going to change my mind, so—"

The doctor sighed deeply and sank down onto the bed. "Your wife," he said, watching Jess carefully, "has been found."

For a moment, Jess simply stared at the doctor blankly. Then he took a step forward. A wild torrent of emotions battered his heart. He was almost afraid to hear the rest of what Marshall had to tell him. "When?" His voice caught and broke. "Is she all right?" He held his breath, waiting for the doctor's answer.

Marshall pulled in a deep breath, hesitating for a moment. Glancing away from Jess, he continued in a faltering voice. "Not . . . exactly, I'm afraid." A look at Jess's stricken face made him hastily add, "She's in a hospital in New York. There was a fire and she was injured."

"A fire?" Absently, Jess began to rub his wounded arm just above the bandage. "What kind of fire? where? how badly is she—"

Marshall held up a restraining hand. "I don't know very much, I'm afraid. A messenger showed up at the church office early this morning. Apparently a doctor at the hospital in New York sent him without knowing that you'd been wounded and were here at home. One of the deacons asked me to tell you." With an apologetic glance, he added, "I'm sorry I didn't tell you as soon as I got here, but I knew you'd insist on going to her right away, and I wanted to be sure you were able."

He shook his head in resignation, "You're not, of course, but I see I might just as well save my breath."

Jess felt his pulse skip, then start to hammer crazily. "You don't know anything more about how she is?"

The doctor shook his head. "All I know is that she's alive. It seems she saved a boy's life in a factory fire. She must have been unconscious, at least for a time, because it was the boy who had the doctor send for you. The message said only that she'd been overcome by smoke and . . . hit by a falling crossbeam."

Jess was unable to draw a deep breath. "Then . . . it could be serious," he said softly, more to himself than to the doctor.

Marshall held out his hands in a gesture of helplessness. "I wish I could tell you more, but I just don't know."

Jess walked quickly to the bedroom door, opened it, and called for Mackenzie; then he went to the clothes closet. He was surprised at how wobbly his legs were and hoped he didn't look as pale as he felt.

Rising from the bed, Marshall walked over to him. "Here," he said, handing him a small white envelope. "Take these with you." When Jess looked down at the envelope in his hand, the doctor explained dryly, "Pain pills. Something tells me you may be glad for them later."

After he closed his medical bag and started toward the door, he turned back. "You have one of the doctors up there take a look at that arm if you're away for any length of time, do you hear?"

Jess nodded. "I will, George. Oh—do you happen to know the name of the boy, the one Kerry rescued from the fire?"

The doctor thought for a moment. "Fitzgerald, I believe. Little fellow, the messenger said. Lost his mother in the fire."

He took a few steps toward Jess, grasping his hand for a long moment. "You'll have my prayers, Pastor. God go with you."

Within moments after Marshall left, both Mackenzie and Molly came into the room. The anxious frown on the housekeeper's

168

face and the expectant, half-smile on the caretaker's told Jess the doctor had already given them the news about Kerry.

"I see you've heard?"

Both nodded and started to speak in unison. Mackenzie, however, simply lifted his shoulders in resignation as Molly overrode his words. "I'll be packing a case for the lass while you get ready to leave, Jess. She'll be needing fresh clothes, no doubt, once she's . . . at herself again." She sniffed and turned to Mackenzie. "You can pack for Jess, and be quick about it," she ordered, moving to leave the room.

"Molly—"

Jess's soft voice stopped her, and she turned back.

"Our girl will be all right," he said quietly. "I'm sure of it."

Molly studied his frightened eyes for a moment, then squared her shoulders and lifted her chin. "Of course she'll be all right, lad," she replied evenly. "She'll be prefectly fine in no time."

Jess smiled weakly at her, wondering if she realized how her mouth trembled when she answered.

CHAPTER TWENTY

At the time Jess's train was nearing New York, Casey-Fitz was chewing his knuckles in a hospital room in the same city, watching the silent and frighteningly still Kerry. Her eyes were shut; her breathing sounded peacefully regular. The doctors said she was in a deep sleep—a coma, they called it.

Casey thought it must be something more than sleep, though, for she wouldn't open her eyes at all, even when he tried to talk to her. For two days, ever since the fire, he had held her hand, sometimes squeezing it ever so gently. He had sung to her, talked to her—indeed had done everything he could think of to awaken her. But still she slept.

The previous afternoon he finally asked the doctor if someone shouldn't let her husband, Mr. Jess, know about her being hurt. The doctor and his assistant promised they would. So far, though, Mr. Jess hadn't come—and surely if he knew, he would have been here by now.

Finally, Casey got up from the chair where he'd been sitting beside the bed for the last few hours. He leaned close to study her face, wanting to be certain she wasn't beginning to wake up.

171

After a moment, he touched her lightly on the forehead and quietly tiptoed from the room.

He decided not to wait any longer. While she was still sleeping, he would go back to the flat. There was an envelope hidden in his mum's Bible that contained a bit of coin they had been saving since the trip over. It was to be the start of their house fund. He would use it now to find help in locating Kerry's giant-husband.

As he walked up the cobbled street toward the flat, he decided to ask Mr. Flaherty for advice. He seemed a kind-hearted man. In fact, Mum had once told him if he ever needed help when she wasn't about, to go see Mr. Flaherty. He was old, she had said, and a mite sick, so he was always in his room. Perhaps Mr. Flaherty could tell him what to do.

The thought of his mum made his eyes burn. He rubbed them fiercely as he turned the last corner on the way to the flat. He mustn't think about her now. Mum was gone, and there was nothing he could do for her. But Kerry was still alive, and he must help her in any way he could. Later, he would think about his mum. When he was sure he had plenty of time to cry, he would think about her.

He began to walk faster, then broke into a run.

Kerry wondered why she hurt so badly; her entire body seemed to be one tight ball of pain. Even her eyes ached with the effort of turning her head first to one side, then the other. Lying still, barely breathing, she waited for the room to stop swaying. Her stomach felt uneasy, as if she might be sick at any moment.

She closed her eyes again. It took too much effort to keep them open. Molly would be calling her a slugabed this morning for sure . . .

Molly. Her eyes flew open, this time focusing more clearly on the room. Molly wasn't here; no one was here. She glanced around, trying to remember, trying to identify her surroundings.

Casey-Fitz—and Maureen. Where are they? Painfully, unwillingly, she remembered. There had been a fire . . . a burning building . . . Maureen had been inside. Then Casey-Fitz . . . surrounded by flames, fire everywhere . . . a blow on her head and the lad's frightened eyes . . .

Where was he? "Casey-Fitz?" She whispered his name, pushed herself up, and leaned heavily on her elbows as she looked with bewilderment around the unfamiliar room.

Her head began to pound like a bellows, and she squeezed her eyes shut once more, only for a moment, willing herself not to be sick. She tried to sit up. Twisting herself to the side of the bed, she tightly hugged her shoulders while pulling in deep, ragged breaths.

The room spun slowly about her, then stopped. A hospital room, that's what it was. There were medicines on the table beside her, a pan, a pitcher, some towels—

The door was ajar and she could hear voices out in the hall. Men were talking. She started to call out to them but stopped when she heard their words.

". . . Some famous Northern preacher, the paper said. Shot him and his secretary both."

"Senator Forbrush, you say? He's the one rumored to be such a crook, you know."

"Apparently he deserved his reputation. He was wounded, too. The preacher used to be at West Point, did you see that?"

"Um-hm. The chaplain. Andrew Dalton's son—remember him, the labor union attorney? Wonder what it was all about. The paper didn't say much."

The voices moved on down the hall, leaving Kerry staring at the door, her eyes wild, her heart going crazy. It had to be Jess. It couldn't be anyone else but Jess. He's been shot? By Senator Forbrush? And Charles—but Charles had been here with me in New York until—

She forced her legs over the side of the bed, then waited for her head to clear and cease its relentless pounding. When the pain refused to go away, she gritted her teeth together and pressed her feet to the floor. Standing up, she nearly fell to her knees with the wave of nausea that assaulted her without warning. Grabbing the table beside the bed, she closed her eyes, waiting.

I've got to get out of here . . . I've got to go to Jess. No, first I'll find Casey-Fitz and Maureen. Maureen. Maureen is dead.

How did she know that? She shook her head and began to walk toward a closet on the other side of the room. She would get dressed, then look for Casey-Fitz. They would go to Jess together.

The only thing in the closet was a scorched, foul-smelling dress, a blackened, torn remnant with part of the skirt ripped away. Her dress. Her shoes were there, but no cloak—not even a shawl. How could she go outside without a wrap? For that matter, how could she go anywhere in that dress?

Kerry turned and started back to the bed. She must think. She would sit down on the bed, wait for the pain in her head to go away, and then she would think what to do.

She got as far as the table before the room tilted. From very far away, she heard a buzzing sound which grew constantly louder until it exploded into a roar. She groped for the table, missed, tried to reach the bed, then fell into a heap on the floor.

Casey took the steps to the hospital entrance two at a time, patting the envelope inside his pocket to assure himself that the money was still there. Mr. Flaherty had been asleep, so he hadn't been able to get any advice from him. Unwilling to stay away from Kerry any longer, he had hurried from the flat and ran all the way back to the hospital, intent upon finding someone to help him get word to Mr. Jess.

A nurse tried to stop him as he sped down the hall, but he brushed her off and zigzagged away from her, darting toward Kerry's room.

As he entered, he saw the empty bed. Confused, he stopped and looked around. Then he saw her lying on the floor like a broken doll.

He cried out, ran to her, fell to his knees, and began tugging at her shoulder. When she didn't move, he hauled himself quickly to his feet and ran into the hall shouting for help.

At first he saw no one except a bearded giant of a man in a black suit with his arm in a sling. The man was walking toward him, but he wasn't Kerry's doctor so Casey continued to call for help.

He crossed the hall and peered into room after room, trying to find a doctor. Finally, he found a nurse and grabbed her hand to take her to Kerry.

At the same time, the big man in the black suit began walking faster and had almost reached Kerry's room. He stared hard at Casey and the nurse. When he got to the door of the room, reaching it at the same time Casey did, he looked at the boy again, then glanced at the number of the room on the door. Casey saw him blink and thought he looked afraid. The boy instinctively stepped aside, and followed the man and the nurse into the room.

The minute Casey saw the man stop and stare at Kerry lying limply on the floor, he knew who he was. The giant man's face took on a terrible expression. For an instant, Casey thought the man would fall to the floor himself. Instead, he dropped to his knees beside her and with his free hand began to touch her hair, her shoulder, then her hair again, all the while murmuring her name.

"Kerry . . . beloved . . . It's all right now, Kerry . . . Everything is going to be all right now, little love . . ."

Casey heard the big man make an awful choking sound as he raised his desperate eyes to the nurse who knelt and took Kerry's hand to check her pulse. With a quick glance of alarm, she jumped up and ran quickly from the room, calling for the doctor.

Casey stood in silence, staring at Kerry and the man beside her, who continued to stroke her hair and murmur to her as if he thought she could hear him. When the doctor finally came running into the room, followed by the nurse, Casey watched them all hover about Kerry. Unnoticed, he then turned and quietly left the room to stand outside the door and wait.

CHAPTER TWENTY-ONE

Jess supposed he had irritated the doctor—certainly he had offended the maidenly nurse's sensibilities—by his insistence that someone find him a rocking chair large enough to hold both himself and Kerry.

She had awakened once, but only for a moment. She hadn't even seen him, he was sure, since they'd banished him to the corner of the room so they could tend to her. The doctor assured him that she would be all right, that she was no longer in a coma but had simply passed out from weakness. She would probably sleep for hours under the medication he had given her. It was then that Jess made his unusual request.

At first, the doctor gave him a look that plainly said he considered the young Mrs. Dalton's husband to be decidedly odd. Never one to be much concerned about how he appeared to others, Jess explained.

"She's been through—a nightmare. And we've been apart for days. At home, when she's upset, I always . . . rock her, by the fire. Please—I just want her to wake up knowing she's safe. She's been frightened for so long."

In the end, the nurse surprised Jess. She followed Dr. Rand out of the room without so much as a backward glance, and returned a few moments later accompanied by two young doctors who, between them, caried a large, extremely comfortable-looking rocking chair.

"If you'll just settle yourself and your wife there, Mr. Dalton," the nurse instructed in a no-nonsense manner, inclining her head toward the rocking chair, "I'll tuck a cover around her to keep her nice and warm. Oh—here, let's put this about her shoulders first." To Jess's great surprise, she produced a soft-looking, light blue shawl from beneath her arm. "Borrowed it from another patient," she said sheepishly.

She waited while Jess shrugged out of his suit coat and then helped him gently drape the shawl around Kerry's slim shoulders. He gathered Kerry up and settled her onto his lap, wedging her small form awkwardly between his good arm and his wounded one.

"Gracious, isn't she a little thing?" she clucked, standing back to admire her work.

Jess looked up into her plain, kindly face and smiled his gratitude. "I can't thank you enough for understanding."

The nurse studied the two of them for a moment with an unfathomable expression, then seemed to mentally shake herself back to business. "I'll be around most of the night if you should need me, Mr. Dalton," she said, turning and walking briskly out of the room.

Assuming the little boy he'd seen outside Kerry's room was the Fitzgerald lad, Jess now wondered where he'd gone and wished he had thought to ask the nurse about him. He wanted to talk with him, to learn more about the fire and what exactly had happened. But the boy disappeared shortly after they found Kerry passed out on the floor. Perhaps a relative had come to get him in the meantime.

He looked down at the elfin face he loved more than life. For what seemed like the first time in days, he was able to take a deep breath of relief. Pressing his lips gently against her cheek, he drew her as close as possible against his warmth, coaxing her head more comfortably onto his chest as he began to rock slowly and evenly. He rocked without ceasing for a long time, until he, too, fell asleep.

Kerry knew she was dreaming—dreaming that she was safely wrapped in Jess's arms, sitting on his lap in their rocking chair, warm, secure, and finally together again.

It was such a beautiful dream she wanted to keep it exactly as it was. She lifted one hand to be sure her eyes were closed, and when she realized they weren't, she blinked once, then again.

With the same hand, she touched his dear, beloved face, brushing her fingertips lightly against his beard and touching his lips, feeling his warm breath. Suddenly, his eyes opened, and he quickly caught her hand against his lips and kissed it ever so gently. His smile was soft with love and tenderness.

"Jess . . . is it a dream I'm having?"

He cherished her with his eyes. "No, little one, you're not dreaming. It's very real. You're safe, and I'm here, and everything is going to be all right now."

Kerry stared at him, afraid he might disappear any moment; she then looked around the darkened room. When she returned her attention to Jess, her gaze focused on his wounded arm with a soft little gasp of remembrance. "You were shot—I heard someone in the hall talking . . ."

He nodded quickly, then pressed a finger over her lips. "I'm all right, though. It was nothing serious."

She thought for a moment. "They said—Senator Forbrush shot you?"

Again he nodded his head. "It was him all the time, Kerry. He was behind—everything." He brushed one limp curl away from her face before going on. "He's quite mad. Apparently, he had some delusion about my usurping his power. He somehow concentrated all his hatred and prejudice on me; getting me out of Washington had become a kind of sick obsession with him, as though eliminating me would also eliminate any threat to him." He shook his head. "The rest of those—savages—worked for Forbrush."

"Charles!" she said suddenly. "Charles tried to take me somewhere—"

"Yes, love, I know," he quickly hushed her with a light kiss. "And I'll never forgive myself for trusting you to him. I might have lost you forever."

He looked so thoroughly miserable that Kerry couldn't bear it. She drew his head down and framed his face between her hands. "You only sent me away to protect me, Jess. You can't be blaming yourself for that."

He said nothing but simply savored her touch on his face.

"And Charles was working—for Senator Forbrush, too?" She didn't wait for him to answer, but let her thoughts tumble out in a confused rush of words. "Poor, awkward Charles. I shouldn't have thought he had a mean bone in him. He's always been odd, but I would have thought him only a weak man, at the very worst."

"He was being blackmailed by Forbrush and his henchmen," Jess told her. Seeing her look of astonishment, he nodded. "I'll tell you everything tomorrow, love," he promised quietly, "when you're stronger. You rest now."

"But it's truly over, Jess?" she asked worriedly, her eyes large and smudged with shadows.

"Yes, love. It's truly over. All of it. We can go home whenever you're well enough to travel." He thought for a moment, then added, "If you don't want to go back to Washington, though, I'll understand. We'll find another place."

"It doesn't matter, Jess," she said tiredly. "I don't care at all where I am, just so long as you're there with me."

"Molly told me how you were treated by some of the women, Kerry, and you don't have to go through that—"

She interrupted him with a small, dismissing motion of her hand. "Doesn't matter," she said groggily. "That all seems so unimportant now in light of everything else that's happened." She yawned, then made an effort to rouse herself. "Besides, I can deal with that in my own way." She gave him a sly little smilte. "Perhaps I'll have a bit of help from Adeline Corbett, as well."

For a moment, she looked as though she were about to drop off to sleep again, and Jess attempted to make her as comfortable as possible in his one-armed embrace. Suddenly, she sat up. "Casey-Fitz!" she exclaimed, instantly alert. "Where is he, Jess?"

"Casey-Fitz?" he repeated with a puzzled frown.

She nodded, her eyes glinting with agitation. "The boy, the little lad—did you see him?"

"Oh—yes. Well, he's gone home, I suppose. Probably left during all the commotion after we found you lying on the floor. Don't you remember, darling? You fainted and fell."

She began to shake her head in distress. "But he saved my life, Jess! We must thank him—and help him somehow."

"Saved your life? I was told that you saved his life."

"Oh, no—that's not true. He ran into the building to find his mother, and I panicked and went after him. But something fell on me, I think, and that's the last thing I remember. It had to be Casey-Fitz, I'm sure, who got us both out of there." Her eyes clouded with sadness when she asked abruptly. "Maureen's dead, isn't she?"

"His mother? Yes, I'm afraid she is, dear. Doesn't the boy have anyone else? What about his father?"

"No one," she answered softly. "His father is dead, too; he died coming over from Ireland. The poor mite is completely alone. Oh, Jess—think of what he did. He went into that burning building with the one thought of saving his mother—instead, because I needed help, he saved me."

"But, Kerry, he probably wouldn't have been able to get to his mother anyway." His gaze swept her face; seeing the pallor of her skin, he frowned with concern.

"Still, don't you see the terrible choice the lad had to make?" she insisted. "In the time it took to save me, he might have found his mother. Oh, Jess—if you knew Casey-Fitz, you'd know that possibility must have occurred to him. Yes, he stayed with me . . ." Her words drifted off as the enormity of her own statement settled over her.

Jess's countenance stilled, too, as his thoughts focused on the significance of what she'd told him. Something began to dawn at the back of his mind, a subtle, rising glint of understanding.

"Jess? What is it?"

He blinked, then said thoughtfully, "I think I could learn a thing or two from your young friend, love."

"What do you mean, Jess?"

He leaned his head against the back of the rocking chair for a moment, then sat forward again. "Casey-Fitz was faced with the choice of spending himself in search of a possibility—or reacting to the immediate need, that of saving your life—and his own, in the process."

He waited, thinking, then went on. "Sometimes, we drain ourselves trying to accomplish the impossible—or at least the unlikely—when what we need to do is take care of the need at hand." He nodded his head slowly, and a small, somewhat rueful smile touched his lips. "Your Casey-Fitz did the immediate thing. That's a lesson that comes hard to me—but one I most desperately need to learn, I fear."

At her puzzled glance, he touched his index finger lightly to the tip of her nose and said, "Let's just say that in the future, instead of concentrating on that distant mountain I'm always trying to move, I'm going to see about clearing the road of a few small stones that are in the way."

She nodded slowly with understanding. "I wish we could start with the boy. Oh, Jess—you should see the place he's living in. It's only a little hole of a room—dark and cold and hardly furnished at all. And he has barely enough to eat."

She clenched her hands together in despair. "They were so kind to me, Jess—the two of them, Maureen and the boy. I was so frightened, and they took me in and shared the little they had with me. And now—"

Tears misted her eyes, but when he tried to comfort her, she sat up even straighter, a frown of dismay creasing her forehead. "Oh, Jess, whatever will he do? And he's such a treasure of a child. Did you see him, did you see his eyes? He loves the old stories and he sings like an angel . . . and do you know, he wants to be a harper, and a doctor, and—"

"Whoa, whoa!" Jess cupped her chin in his hand, smiling at her outburst. "Do you know, Kerry Shannon, that for the very first time since I married you, I do believe I'm jealous?"

She stared at him blankly, then laughed a little. Her expression quickly sobered, however. "Oh, Jess—please try to find him right away. He shouldn't be alone, not now, so soon after losing his mother. And . . . I don't know why I'm so sure, but I believe he's

182

been here with me, ever since the fire."

His eyes questioning, he studied her face for a long moment. "You're really taken with the boy, aren't you, love?"

"You'd understand why if you could spend a bit o' time with him, Jess. He has a way about him. I don't know exactly what it is . . . but he's—special."

He pulled her close to him, wrapping her hand in his and brushing his lips tenderly across her fingers. "Must be the Irish in him," he murmured. "They definitely have a way of stealing one's heart, I'm told."

They sat quietly for a long time, Kerry resting against his warmth, drawing from his strength and his love, each thinking their own thoughts. It was Jess who finally broke the silence.

"Kerry—" he stopped, seemed to make a decision, then went on. "You say the boy's alone?"

Kerry turned to look at him. "Yes—he has no one."

"Perhaps when you're stronger, we could think about—"

She didn't let him finish. "What, Jess?"

"Not now, dear. You have to rest. Later, we'll talk about what we might be able to do for your Casey-Fitz."

She sat up in his arms. "What are you thinking?" Her eyes took on a childlike glint of anticipation. "Jess?"

He pursed his lips thoughtfully and gave her an uncertain look. "Well, you're obviously—fond of the boy. And if he's been hanging around you as much as you think, he must be—attached to you, as well. Perhaps . . ." He left the thought unfinished, and for a moment Kerry thought he was about to drift into one of those mind-wandering, distant moods of his.

Anxious to keep his attention, she prompted. "Perhaps what, Jess?"

His eyes cleared. "Perhaps—later, of course—we could talk with him about—living with us."

She opened her mouth in surprise, then quickly clamped it shut. "Why do we have to wait until later? Why couldn't we talk to him right away?"

"Well, I told you, love, we need to wait until you're stronger."

"I'm perfectly strong enough now," she insisted. "Jess, are you suggesting what I think you are? Are you saying we could take

Casey-Fitz back with us—that is, if he wants to go—that he could stay with us and be . . . our own?"

As always, her quicksilver mind threatened to leave him in the dust, and he found himself mentally groping to catch up with her. "Ah . . . yes . . . yes. I suppose that's what I'm saying, love. If the boy has no one else, perhaps he'd be willing to—adopt us as his parents. What do you think?"

She stared at him for only an instant, then threw her arms around his neck, surprising him with her strength as she kissed him soundly. "I think," she declared fervently, "that you are the most wonderful man alive, Jess Dalton. And I think I love you more than everything."

"I see. Ah . . . does that mean you approve of my idea?"

She nodded her head vigorously. "Will you try to find him now, Jess? Please?"

"Kerry, I don't think the boy is here. Surely he is exhausted and has probably started on his way home by this time."

"But will you just look, Jess?"

He sighed, pretending exasperation, then nodded. "All right. If you'll promise to get back into bed and stay there this time. I'll see if I can find this—treasure of a lad who has so thoroughly charmed you."

Obediently, she started to remove herself from his lap. Just as quickly, he tightened his embrace. "Not so fact, Mrs. Dalton," he said softly. "You'll not start bouncing out of my arms again so soon after finding your way back into them."

He stood then and would have picked her up, but his wounded arm wouldn't hold her. He winced at the pain.

"Jess!" Kerry gasped.

He smiled down at her. "I'm all right; really I am."

He took her arm and led her over to the bed.

He whispered, "I love you . . . more than everything, Kerry, mavourneen."* Then he kissed her breathless and put her gently back to bed.

Casey thought he might as well go back to the flat. Earlier, he had left his hiding place just long enough to peep into Kerry's room. When he saw she was awake and that Jess was holding her on his lap, he quietly, though somewhat reluctantly, returned to the dark little niche around the corner from the supply closet and sank to the floor.

He could leave now; there was no need to hang arond. She wouldn't need him to watch over her any longer. Still he delayed, thinking about how it had been for a while to have someone who needed him. Mum had depended on him, of course, but she was gone now. And since Kerry had needed him so soon after losing his mum, there hadn't been time to feel alone—or lonely.

But Kerry was obviously fine now, so he could be on his way. He needed to go back to the flat and think about what to do. He would have to find work soon. There would be no more piecework from the Bowden factory, of course, since it had been demolished by the fire.

It was just as well. He had always hated doing the piecework. He'd never said anything to his Mum, for she was sad enough without his adding to her pain. But he had promised himself that he would never touch a needle again if he were ever finished with this business.

He thought about going to sea. Perhaps he could get a job on a ship and have a look at other countries. He might even end up back in Ireland for a bit.

He patted his pocket. Sure, and there was enough to get him by until he found work that suited him. He tried to think about it, but the thought of his mum's thin, worried face kept getting mixed up with all the other thoughts in his head. He gave it up for the present.

He propped up his legs, folded his arms on them, and put his head down to rest. At last, he let himself think about his mum. He spent a long time remembering her; finally, he allowed himself to cry.

That was how Jess found him—huddled in a damp, dark corner, his tear-streaked, dirty face propped on his knees, his thin, bony shoulders heaving with sobs.

Casey looked up, his large, brave eyes widening at the sight of Kerry's giant husband standing over him. They studied each other in silence for a long time before Jess reached out a hand to help the lad to his feet. "Will you come with me, son? Kerry and I would like to talk with you . . . about something very important."

Casey looked at the immense hand and then glanced up into the giant's smiling eyes. He hesitated a moment before grasping the outstretched hand and rising from the dark corner.

The giant draped his free arm around the boy's thin, narrow shoulders, and together they walked down the dimly lighted corridor. Once, when the giant glanced down to find the boy's solemn eyes studing him with enormous interest, he smiled an odd little smile and said, seemingly to himself, "Ah, Lord, it seems you went to the trouble of handpicking him, didn't you? Complete with copper curls and shamrock eyes."

He chuckled softly, gave the boy's shoulder a gentle squeeze, then shook his head in wonder as they walked on.

EPILOGUE

April 5, 1865
Richmond, Virginia

Dear Dad and Little Mother . . .

I'm writing this on my birthday, blessed by the assurance that today, as I'm thinking lovingly of you, you are thinking of me and wondering if your roaming boy is alive and well.

Rest yourself, Little Mother, for I'm perfectly fine. I have good news. Though you may hear it long before you read this letter, I want the pleasure of writing down the words to those I love best. The war, you see, is at last about to end.

President Lincoln is in Richmond today, and all the boys are trying to look at him, yours truly included, of course. Word has it that Lee is ready to surrender; his forces are depleted, and his men are starving. It's over—finally over. But, oh, haven't we paid a price.

I've been with General Grant for several weeks now. Somehow, he learned that I'm your son, and we sat for hours one night talking about the years you were together at West Point. You should hear him speak of you, Dad; what respect! And he asked if you're still as pretty and saucy as you were years ago, Little Mother. I told him, of course, that you are! Didn't my eyes bug to learn that our famous Union general was the very same cadet who drove your carriage the day you two were married.

Some say the general had no mind for the military when he was a cadet at the Academy, that he only cared about the horses. Perhaps you'd know about that, Dad; I intend to ask you all about him when I get home, for he's a fascinating fellow. I also sense that he's a sorrowful, lonely man—a man with a bottomless, gentle spirit and a sad, haunted soul.

But no more talk of war. Today is for our memories, especially mine of you. Always, my heart is filled with the two of you and the rich, happy life you've given me. What an incredible, wonderful legacy is mine, thanks to both of you.

I'm remembering that long ago night in New York City when I saw you striding toward me, Dad, down that hospital corridor. I thought you were the biggest man I'd ever seen, and the years have made it abundantly clear that you are every bit the giant I believed you to be.

One of my favorite memories is of the day I stepped off the train in Washington when you and Little Mother took me home with you as your own son. I can still feel the soft wool of my new gray suit and my stiff black shoes and that ridiculous hat I kept for years. Most of all, though, I remember Grandma Molly wrapping me up in her arms as if she'd ordered me special from New York—and Grandpa Mack handing me my own shillelagh, which he said no self-respecting Irishman should ever be without.

Will any of us ever forget the day those two dear souls were wed to each other in your church, Dad, with you reading the service—as best you could, that is, over the sounds of Little Mother's weeping?

Oh, how I loved the both of them—and how endlessly patient they were with me . . . even when I ruined Grandma Molly's shiny waxed floors by chasing Brian Boru across them at top speed . . . or when I filled Grandpa Mack's pipe with nutmeg to see his mustache flap up and down.

And didn't Grandma do exactly what she always told Grandpa Mack she intended—going to the Lord ahead of him to be sure the angels were forewarned that he was on his way. How I miss them now that they're gone.

What a rich man I am, loved ones. Today, I am twenty-seven years old, and I've never lived a day without the security of knowing somebody loves me, more than anything.

I owe both of you so much. You've given me a fine education at West Point, medical school, a grand home, a good life, love— so much love.

And how, Little Mother, could I go searching among my dearest memories without being ever so keenly aware of all the gentle, lovely ways you have fed my Celtic soul? The songs you sang throughout my childhood, the stories you told me, the legends you breathed life into, the poetry and the music—ah, that grand and glorious music.

What a pair the two of you are. I can still see you, Dad, tossing our Little Mother into a snowdrift—just to watch her emerald eyes flash. And never, ever, will I forget the sight of her snuggled on your lap as the two of you rocked in front of the fire, drawing strength and comfort from each other, always so completely, wonderfully, in love.

Pity me, though, when I begin to search for my own love. For how could I ever settle for less than what I've seen between the two of you? May the good Lord bless me with such a love, and I'll never ask for more.

God willing, I'll be home soon, loved ones. For now, at least, I'm tired of doctoring, tired of blood, pain, hopelessness, and death . . . tired of being tired. I have it in my mind to live my dream and go to Ireland once I rest for a bit. I have to go back or I'll never really know myself. I have a need to see where I came from and what it was like. I want to get to know the land and the people so I can choose what to bring home with me and what to finally leave behind.

But first, I'm coming home—coming home to be healed by your love, for nothing but love can heal the wounds this war has inflicted upon me and so many others like me.

Growing up in the circle of such a vast, enormous love—only that has enabled me to walk these battlefields of misery and remain a whole man while keeping a bit of hope for when it's over.

I thank God every day of my life for you, Dad, and you, my adorable Little Mother. I thank you both for the wonderful memories that will forever be a part of me . . . for the shelter of a love as big as all eternity.

I am now and always will be—

Your devoted son,
Casey Fitzgerald Dalton

GLOSSARY

avourneen/mavourneen: my darling

alannah: endearment for young child

asthore: my love; my beloved

bodhran: drum made of goat skin stretched over a wooden frame

clairseach: ancient wire-strung harp

cuisle mo chroid: pulse of my heart

fianna: legendary band of professional Irish warriors bound by rules of chivalry, sworn to fight for the king against foreign foes and for peace among the clans within the realm.

gombeen men: unscrupulous money lenders

go sabhala Dia sinn: God save (help) us

ochone: exclamation of distress; "Oh, dear!" "Goodness!" "Alas!"

Orange Peel: nickname Daniel O'Connell gave to the British prime minister, Sir Robert Peel

puca: goblin

wirra: exclamation; "Oh!"